A PARADISE ON EARTH

"I cannot take you with me," she asserted. "We mermaids swim alone and no man may follow us. It is forbidden."

She pulled away from him and dived swiftly, so that he saw a flash of shapely ankle before she vanished into the depths. Instantly he dived as well and felt a moment's panic because he could not see her in the dark blue water.

At last he sensed her gliding past him as though she was indeed the mermaid she had claimed to be. This time he was taking no chances. He put on a spurt and caught up with her, seizing her waist.

Above them the water was pale from the light above. Up and up they climbed until they broke the surface and the sunshine streamed over them again. At first they laughed into each other's eyes, but suddenly they stopped laughing and trod water, looking astonished at what had come over them.

The shore was so distant as to be almost invisible. Overhead the blue sky was empty and the sea stretched far away into the distance. They might have been completely alone in the world with no one to see what they did next.

Slowly John drew her towards him. Her arms enfolded his neck and the next moment he was kissing her, and she was kissing him.

The Barbara Cartland Pink Collection

Titles in this series

A PARADISE ON EARTH

BARBARA CARTLAND

Barbaracartland.com Ltd

Printed and bound in Great Britain by
CLE Print Ltd. of St Ives, Cambridgeshire.

THE BARBARA CARTLAND PINK COLLECTION

Barbara Cartland was the most prolific bestselling author in the history of the world. She was frequently in the Guinness Book of Records for writing more books in a year than any other living author. In fact her most amazing literary feat was when her publishers asked for more Barbara Cartland romances, she doubled her output from 10 books a year to over 20 books a year, when she was 77.

She went on writing continuously at this rate for 20 years and wrote her last book at the age of 97, thus completing 400 books between the ages of 77 and 97.

Her publishers finally could not keep up with this phenomenal output, so at her death she left 160 unpublished manuscripts, something again that no other author has ever achieved.

Now the exciting news is that these 160 original unpublished Barbara Cartland books are ready for publication and they will be published by Barbaracartland.com exclusively on the internet, as the web is the best possible way to reach so many Barbara Cartland readers around the world.

The 160 books will be published monthly and will be numbered in sequence.

The series is called the Pink Collection as a tribute to Barbara Cartland whose favourite colour was pink and it became very much her trademark over the years.

The Barbara Cartland Pink Collection is published only on the internet. Log on to www.barbaracartland.com to find out how you can purchase the books monthly as they are published, and take out a subscription that will ensure that all subsequent editions are delivered to you by mail order to your home.

If you do not have access to a computer you can write for information about the Pink Collection to the following address :

Barbara Cartland.com Ltd.
240 High Road,
Harrow Weald,
Harrow HA3 7BB
United Kingdom.

Telephone & fax: +44 (0)20 8863 2520

THE LATE DAME BARBARA CARTLAND

Barbara Cartland who sadly died in May 2000 at the age of nearly 99 was the world's most famous romantic novelist who wrote 723 books in her lifetime with worldwide sales of over 1 billion copies and her books were translated into 36 different languages.

As well as romantic novels, she wrote historical biographies, 6 autobiographies, theatrical plays, books of advice on life, love, vitamins and cookery. She also found time to be a political speaker and television and radio personality.

She wrote her first book at the age of 21 and this was called *Jigsaw*. It became an immediate bestseller and sold 100,000 copies in hardback and was translated into 6 different languages. She wrote continuously throughout her life, writing bestsellers for an astonishing 76 years. Her books have always been immensely popular in the United States, where in 1976 her current books were at numbers 1 & 2 in the B. Dalton bestsellers list, a feat never achieved before or since by any author.

Barbara Cartland became a legend in her own lifetime and will be best remembered for her wonderful romantic novels, so loved by her millions of readers throughout the world.

Her books will always be treasured for their moral message, her pure and innocent heroines, her good looking and dashing heroes and above all her belief that the power of love is more important than anything else in everyone's life.

"Love truly makes the world go round and the universe as well."

Barbara Cartland

PROLOGUE
1855

It was cold in the Barrack Hospital, but at least there was a roof overhead and oil lamps to cast a soft glow. To the wounded men who had endured the freezing voyage over the Black Sea from Balaclava to reach the hospital at Scutari, any shelter was welcome.

The man lying on the low bed barely felt the cold and the filth. Even his terrible pain seemed to reach him from a distance. He was dying, and he knew it.

He thought of his father and brother, both far away in England. He had never been close to them, but he would have liked to speak to them one last time. Now he knew he would never see them again.

He was vaguely aware of a woman kneeling beside his bed, drawing aside the tattered jacket of his uniform that proclaimed him an officer in the Light Brigade. Then the pain became overwhelming and he passed out.

When he came round his condition had improved. Somebody had cleaned him and dressed his wound, although the pain was still severe.

He gradually realised that someone was sitting by his bed, and after a moment he recognised him.

"Robert," he whispered hoarsely.

"That's better, Major," said Sergeant Robert Dale.

He was a burly individual in his thirties, with a broad face that now bore a smile of relief.

"For a while I thought you were gone for good," he said. "I have been thinking that for days now. But there you are, sir! I never thought you would survive charging the Russian guns."

"So many didn't survive it," Major Milton muttered, his eyes closing as the painful memories converged on him.

Six hundred men on horseback, charging down a narrow valley to reach an impossible target! Nearly half of them had been cut down.

"And then when I found you on the boat," Robert Dale continued. "I thought you were going to die at any moment. But I guess you are indestructible, sir."

"I don't feel indestructible," John Milton murmured. "I keep expecting to fall asleep and not wake up. But never mind me. What about your wounds?"

"Not too bad, sir," Robert replied, indicating his bandaged right arm and also his wounded left leg.

He was about to settle down to a discussion of wounds when he saw a woman approaching the bed. She was in her thirties with a thin face and a voice that was gentle but full of authority.

"You must go, now," she ordered. "The Major needs to sleep. You may return tomorrow."

Robert knew who she was. Everyone knew.

"But will he still be alive tomorrow, Miss Nightingale, ma'am?" he asked urgently.

"He will if I have anything to do with it," she answered quietly.

Something in her manner reassured the Sergeant. He walked away without another word.

When he returned next day, it was to find Major John Milton still alive, but with a terrible grey look to his face. Robert began to talk to him in a voice of grim determination, as though, by doing so, he could keep him still in the land of the living. Sometimes the Major roused himself to speak.

"I thought the army would be such an adventure," he mumbled. "I was even glad that I was the younger son, so that I could go off and have 'fun'. I was just a boy then. I thought being in a cavalry regiment meant parading around in a glittering uniform, riding a fine horse, flirting with all the pretty girls."

He fell silent and Robert was silent too, understanding what he could not say. The Crimean War had broken out between Russia and Britain. Eager young soldiers had been shipped out to the action. But, with terrible speed, dreams of adventure had ended in the mud.

"How could they have sent us into that charge?" the Major asked, more like his old self. "Like sheep to the slaughter."

He closed his eyes as though trying to shut out the memory.

"Don't think of it, sir," Robert urged.

"You are right. Talk about yourself. I think you once told me that you come from a family of inn-keepers?"

"That's right, sir. My father owns a Public House in London. He wanted me to go into the trade, but I ran away to join the army. Recently though I have been thinking that being a landlord might suit me."

"Yes, the quiet life now starts to look very attractive," the Major agreed. "If I come through this, I think I will do something peaceful, myself."

He gave a faint grin.

"Maybe I'll try my hand at being a landlord. It could be a good life, standing behind a bar being 'mine host'."

"Now you're making fun of me, sir. Lords such as yourself don't become landlords."

"I am not a Lord."

"I thought you said your father was an Earl?"

"And so I did. He is Earl Milton. And my brother George is Viscount Milton until our father dies, and then he will be the Earl. But I am just John Milton, or 'the Honourable John Milton' on letters."

"But you were brought up as a Lord?" Robert asked, sounding anxious.

"Yes, I was."

"With a big country estate?" Robert added hopefully. His ideas about Lords were being threatened.

"A huge country estate," John reassured him. "Milton Park is a wonderful place, with a deer park and ancient oaks."

"I wonder you could ever bear to leave it, sir."

John did not feel able to tell him that he had fled his cold, dismissive father and his selfish arrogant brother. In their society he had felt excluded, and had been glad to leave them behind. In Robert Dale, a man he would once have been taught to despise as beneath him, he had found more true warmth and friendship than he had ever known in his family.

"It was big," he murmured. "Too big. There was no chance to get to know anyone properly. An inn would be – friendly. And people would smile when they saw you."

The Sergeant stared. Great Lords (for so he still thought of John Milton) were supposed to be above caring for such things. Then he realised that the Major must be feverish, which accounted for his rambling thoughts.

"I expect you would like to sleep now, sir," he suggested, rising. "I'll come again tomorrow."

As he moved away he saw Miss Nightingale standing close enough to have heard his final words.

"I am afraid you may not return here," she said softly. "We have an outbreak of cholera, and the fewer people who move around the hospital the better. But I expect you'll be leaving soon anyway."

She indicated his arm and leg, both wounded, but neither badly enough to incapacitate him.

"Yes, ma'am," he agreed, awed by the great lady.

"Then you are one of the lucky ones," she said. "More people die of disease in this place than of their wounds."

"The Major – " he exclaimed in alarm.

"Pray for him," Florence Nightingale replied simply.

The following day Sergeant Dale was shipped out of Scutari and invalided home without seeing John Milton again, or being able to obtain any news about him.

CHAPTER ONE
1858

Cecilia ran as hard as her legs would take her. If only she could only reach the house and run up the stairs before Sir Stewart caught her. She could hear him now, puffing and gasping as he chased her through the garden. He was getting close, but too much alcohol and rich food had left him out of condition. She might still escape.

But as she reached the trees she stumbled and then he was upon her, grabbing her arms and pulling her against him.

"Why do you run away from me?" he demanded, breathing beer fumes over her.

"Because I cannot bear the sight of you," she cried, frantically turning her head away.

She felt sick with disgust, not only at the smell of the man, but at the sight of him too. His red, fleshy face was loathsome, but more loathsome still was his heavy, slack body, held against hers, pressing her back against a tree.

"Get away from me," she screamed. "Don't touch me."

"Come now, you don't fool me," he wheezed. "I know very well that this display of reluctance is only to increase my ardour. But there's no need, you know. My desire for you is already at fever pitch, and nothing will stop our marriage."

"*I* will stop our marriage," she raged. "I will never marry you. Why can't you understand that?"

He laughed nastily. "Perhaps because it doesn't suit me to understand it. I am your guardian and I wish to marry you. I have applied to myself, and I have granted myself permission. So there is nothing left to do but to set the date."

"Except that I will not marry you," she cried.

"You have no choice. You will do as your guardian decrees."

"I'll die first."

"Stop talking nonsense. Our marriage is all settled. I am looking forward to it. Now, how about a little kiss, as a token of your love for me?"

To her horror he pressed his face against hers, so that there was no escape from his heavy, tobacco-stained moustache. She turned her head frantically this way and that, just managing to escape his mouth.

At last, using all her strength, she succeeded in pushing him away. He stumbled back and fell over a log that lay on the ground just behind him.

His eyes kindled with rage.

"Why you – "

Cecilia heard no more. Picking up her skirts, she fled through the trees into the house and up the stairs to her own room. There she leaned against the door and burst into loud sobs.

She could hardly believe that she had been brought to this. Only six months earlier she had been living a happy life, the darling of her father, Charles Reynolds, a very wealthy merchant. She had loved him dearly and since her mother's death, five years earlier, they had been everything to each other.

Dearest Papa had been perfect in every way but one, and that was his yearning for a title. He had longed to see his daughter raised to the ranks of the aristocracy, and when Sir Stewart Paxton had arrived in their orbit, he had been overwhelmed.

It was not easy for a merchant's daughter to achieve a brilliant match. In London Mr. Reynolds had been horribly snubbed. Even his wealth could not buy him admission to the really fashionable places, where the great Lords and Ladies met and played.

At his home on the south coast things were easier. Brighton had been fashionable ever since the Prince Regent had held court there in his extravagant pavilion. Those days were long gone. The spendthrift Prince had become a spendthrift King and had died twenty-eight years ago.

But the well-off and the lower ranks of the aristocracy had continued to travel to Brighton in the summer, to bathe in the sea and enjoy the many amusements set out for their pleasure.

Here Mr. Reynolds might hope to achieve some minor social success for his daughter. When he met Sir Stewart he thought that here, at last, was the title he wanted for Cecilia.

Cecilia had seen it differently. To her, Sir Stewart was a vulgarian with no fine feelings and a profound greed for money. He flattered her father, inveigled him into card games and almost always won. Cecilia was certain that he was cheating.

He was not at all the sort of man she wanted. Like any young girl she dreamed of a Knight in shining armour, a handsome young man who would court her romantically, sweep her off her feet into a glittering fantasy, and adore her for ever.

There were plenty of young men casting wistful eyes at her, attracted by her shining honey-blonde hair, elegant figure and large blue eyes. But her father dismissed them all.

"They are only after your money, my dear," he assured her. "They know I will leave you a large fortune."

"Oh, Papa, I am sure you are wrong," she riposted, remembering one young man who had held her hand for just a little longer than was proper, and another who had gazed longingly into her eyes.

Not that she mentioned these incidents to her father. She had a feeling that he would not see them in the same blissful light as herself.

"You leave these matters to me, my dear," Papa had asserted, patting her hand. "Rely on your father to choose the perfect husband for you."

But his idea of the perfect husband turned out to be Sir Stewart. When Cecilia heard the news, she laughed out loud. Surely Papa was joking. But, to her horror, he was serious.

"You will bear a title," he urged. "Lady Paxton. Her Ladyship. Just think of that!"

"Thinking about it makes me feel ill," she had replied.

Papa had been angry with her for one of the few times that she could remember. He had stormed off and Cecilia had fled the house, seeking refuge with Mrs. Alice Baines.

Alice had been her nurse for several years. When she had left, five years earlier, to marry George Baines, a butcher, she had moved only a few miles away and Cecilia had continued to visit her. After Sir Stewart began pestering her, Cecilia called more often.

Mrs. Baines calmed her down, gave her good advice on how to deal with Papa, and sent her home ever more determined to hold out. And Mrs. Baines's advice had been so good that when Cecilia's father died, she was still unmarried.

But her relief was short-lived. In his will, made a few

9

days before his death, Mr. Reynolds had appointed Sir Stewart as her guardian. In a week she had found herself forcibly moved into Sir Stewart's London house, so that there was no escape from his unceasing importunities.

"No escape," Cecilia murmured to herself now. "I am a prisoner here. Oh, what shall I do?"

She listened at the door, terrified in case Sir Stewart came after her. But to her relief she heard him leaving by the front door. A moment later there was the sound of a carriage driving away.

Instantly she sprang to life, seizing her bonnet, throwing on a cloak and slipping out of the door. In the corridor she heard footsteps approaching from an upper floor, and hurried down the stairs to avoid being seen. She slipped out of a side door and hurried until she reached the street. To her relief she found a cab quickly, and gave Mrs. Baines's address.

Cecilia reached the shop to find Mr. Baines serving behind the counter. He waved when he saw her.

"Go right along to the back," he called. "She'll be so pleased to see you and tell you our good news."

Mrs. Baines greeted her with ecstasy and immediately confided that she and Mr. Baines were expecting their third child.

"Motherhood really suits you!" Cecilia exclaimed in delight.

"I look forward to seeing you with little ones of your own, my pretty, when you've found the right husband. Is that monster still tormenting you?"

"Oh, Alice, it's terrible. He gets worse and worse. How could Papa have brought himself to leave me in his clutches?"

"Your father was a good man in many ways," Alice sighed. "But give him the sniff of a title and he became a bit cracked in the head. But I'm really glad to see you. I thought Sir Stewart would stop you visiting me."

"He tries to. I slip out secretly. I even have to avoid my maid because she's a spy for him. He dismissed my faithful Jane and forced me to have a maid of his choosing. Her name is Harriet and she's always watching me and then sneaking off to him.

"He says she is a 'high class maid' and I shall need her for when I am 'moving in court circles' as he puts it. But actually she's useless. It's lucky that you and Jane taught me to do everything for myself.

"Oh, Alice, my life is a nightmare. I am a virtual prisoner in the house. That horrible man says it's because we are in mourning for Papa, but he just doesn't want me to meet anyone else. I have to escape. But how? And where would I go?"

"Why, you could come to us," Alice said at once.

"You are a darling, but I couldn't impose on you."

"You wouldn't be imposing at all," said Mr. Baines, coming in from the shop. "It wouldn't be a good idea for you to stay for long, because he might find you. But if you do escape, you must come to us first and we'll see what's to be done next."

"You are both so kind," Cecilia sighed. "It means so much to me to know that I can throw myself on your mercy, but I am sure – that is, I hope – that I won't need to run away. Sir Stewart will see sense. I just have to be firm."

She continued to try and convince herself of this all the way home and even managed to find a little reassurance in it. She was lucky in managing to slip into the house unseen, but when she was half way up the stairs, her luck ended.

"Where have you been?"

Sir Stewart's voice was like the crack of a whip. She turned to see him standing at the foot of the stairs, scowling.

"I said where have you been?" he repeated nastily.

"Anywhere as long as it's out of this house," she told him defiantly.

"Do not bandy words with me, girl. I demand to know where you've been."

"And I refuse to tell you."

He climbed the stairs until they were face to face.

"Have you been meeting some man?" he demanded.

"No. And that is all I am going to tell you."

"I don't believe you. You are arranging secret assignations, aren't you? Admit it."

"I have nothing to admit."

"Then why do you creep out alone. A decent woman takes her maid with her."

"That nasty creature you set to spy on me? I detest her almost as much as I detest you. I refuse to answer any more questions. What I do is none of your affair?"

"You are my promised wife – " he shouted.

"That is a lie. The only promise I ever made was to be rid of you as soon as possible and that will be very soon. I shall be twenty-one before long, and then I will leave this house, and you will have to account for what you have done with my money. I do not think you will find that very easy, but you won't cheat me as you cheated my father."

For a moment she thought he would hit her. His face became purple with rage and he drew a sharp breath.

Then he seemed to force himself to be calm.

"I will deal with you later," he said hoarsely. "For now, go and prepare for dinner. We are entertaining."

"And who will the guests be this time? More of your drinking friends?"

"The Reverend Shotton will be our guest, so please

behave yourself."

Cecilia ran the rest of the way upstairs. It was no relief to her to find that the guest was a clergyman, for the Reverend Shotton was a man cut from the same cloth as Sir Stewart. Beneath the trappings of his vocation he was vulgar and coarse, both of which qualities he made worse by assuming an air of unctuous piety.

Harriet appeared, ready to help her dress for dinner.

"I have put out two dresses that would be suitable, miss" she announced primly.

Cecilia looked at the two gowns and immediately rejected them both.

"They are too low-cut," she said. "It would not be proper for me to wear them while I am in mourning for my father."

"It is Sir Stewart's wish that you look your best tonight," Harriet replied in a harsh voice.

Cecilia's eyes flashed with anger.

"Do not try to dictate to me!" she cried. "I will decide what is proper for me to wear. Not you and certainly not Sir Stewart."

Crossing to her wardrobe, she sorted through her gowns until she found one of dark blue silk, cut high in the bosom.

Harriet's mouth hardened.

"That is not what Sir Stewart wishes you to wear," she said coldly.

Cecilia was now in control of her temper and answered with deceptive sweetness,

"But Harriet, Mr. Shotton would wish me to dress demurely. He is a man of stern, moral rectitude."

Since Harriet knew that this was untrue, but could hardly say so, she was left floundering, while Cecilia

13

proceeded to don the austere garment. The only decoration she permitted herself was a pair of jet ear-rings that had belonged to her mother.

Then she walked slowly downstairs to sit in the library until the evening should begin.

Sir Stewart found her and scowled when he saw how she was attired.

"Harriet tells me that you are being difficult about this evening."

"On the contrary, I am behaving very properly in dressing with restraint," she informed him coolly.

He appeared to be struggling with his temper. At last he managed to control himself and assumed a smile that sickened her with its falsity.

"Let us not argue," he said. "I have brought you a gift and I merely wanted you to be able to display it properly."

Cecilia said nothing.

"Don't you want to know what the gift is?" he asked in a wheedling tone.

"I do not wish to receive anything from you," she said firmly.

"Come now, every girl likes presents."

"That depends on who gives them. I want nothing from you."

He seemed to speak through gritted teeth.

"Don't you think you might make an effort to be a little pleasant?"

"I shall be perfectly pleasant to our guest when he arrives, but I have nothing to say to you."

"Not even for this?" he asked with a sickening smile, bringing a black velvet box out from behind his back.

He opened it with a flourish, revealing a diamond necklace.

Cecilia regarded him coolly. Obviously she was supposed to be overcome with gratitude, but all she could feel was a cynical suspicion that he had paid for the necklace with *her* money.

"I told you that I want nothing from you," she repeated. "And I meant it."

She turned away from him, but he was after her in a flash, wrapping the necklace around her throat.

"Don't spurn me when I am being so good to you," he squealed angrily.

"Get away from me," she cried, trying to struggle free.

But he was stronger and grasped her with rough hands, turning her to face him and trying to plant a kiss on her face. She almost fainted with disgust. Earlier that day she had merely pushed him off. Now she drew her arm back and landed him a hefty slap on the face, managing at the same time to rake his cheek with her nails, so that the scratches were visible.

"Why you little – !"

But before he could say any more, they heard the sound of the doorbell ringing. The Reverend Shotton had arrived.

"I'll deal with you later," Sir Stewart snarled and pushed past her into the hall to greet his guest.

Cecilia took a deep breath and prepared to endure the evening.

It was a strain, but somehow she survived. Mr. Shotton's gaze fixed at once on the scratches on Sir Stewart's cheek and then to her, in a manner that showed he understood everything.

She suspected that Sir Stewart had enlisted him as an ally and knew it for sure when the clergyman dropped a hint about 'setting the date'. She braced herself for an argument but it did not come. Sir Stewart hastily dismissed the subject with a remark about Cecilia being in mourning.

From which she concluded that he was unwilling to provoke her into open defiance. She felt a twinge of satisfaction at having alarmed him into silence. But she knew it was only for the moment. She could not afford to relax.

As soon as possible she bade them goodnight and left them to their port. Upstairs she paced the floor, unable to go to bed. She knew she would not be able to sleep. Suddenly everything was more serious than she had imagined.

The room seemed to be closing in on her. She had to get out. Peering into the corridor, she looked each way before heading down the stairs. If she went through the conservatory she could slip out into the garden.

But as soon as she entered the conservatory she froze. From behind a clump of tall plants she heard the sound of Sir Stewart's voice.

"So you see how it is. I am in even more dire straits than I thought."

And Mr. Shotton replied,

"Well, you certainly didn't help matters by the amount you lost the other night."

"You are hardly in a position to lecture me," Sir Stewart said roughly, "seeing as it was you who won most of it."

"Well I lost it to someone else straight afterwards," Mr. Shotton said. "So we're neither of us well off."

"And I have to do something fast. I thought I would have her safely married to me by now, but she's an obstinate little baggage. What is more I think there's a man she is slipping out to see. I cannot afford to lose her. She is threatening to set the law on to me when she's twenty-one and that would ruin me, if the creditors don't ruin me first."

"So what do you expect me to do about it?"

"Marry us!"

"But she cannot stand you, if those scratches on your face are anything to go by. She will never consent."

"Then I will damned well do without her consent. She'll come to church whether she likes it or not and then you will marry us."

"You don't expect her to just let you drag her off, do you?" Shotton demanded. "She has plenty of fire in her and she'll yell the place down."

"Not if she is given something to quieten her down first."

There was a silence. Then Mr. Shotton asked,

"Drug her, you mean?"

"Why not? Put an end to her nonsense, once and for all."

"Do not tell me any more. I don't want to hear about it."

"But you will marry us, if you want to be paid the rest of your money."

"I suppose I shall have to. Make it soon."

Cecilia's heart was thundering as she slowly backed out of the conservatory. She could hardly breathe as all her fears converged onto her. She had been playing for time and suddenly there was no time left. If she was to escape at all, it must be tonight.

She forced herself to be calm and to behave normally.

When Harriet came to her room she allowed her to undress her, brush her hair and bid her goodnight.

She sat in darkness while the house grew silent around her. Then she lit a small lamp and took a suitcase from the wardrobe.

Her first idea was to take only the basic necessities. But she soon realised that she did not know where she was going, or how long she might be away. So Cecilia packed as many of her good clothes as she could cram into the case, before pulling out the top drawer of her dressing table.

Inside there was a locked box containing a good deal of money. Her father's generous allowance had been paid to her just before his death and she had kept it, never knowing when she might need money urgently.

Had some part of her always known that this day would come? At any rate, she blessed whichever instinct had led her to save this money, so that now she had enough to escape.

And that was exactly what she was going to do.

She dressed swiftly and looked out into the corridor of the dark, silent house. She resisted the temptation to run, creeping slowly downstairs and into the kitchen.

The cat opened one eye and regarded her sleepily for a moment. Cecilia put a finger to her lips and shook her head. The cat stretched and curled up again as she let herself out of the back door. Now she was in the garden within reach of the gate.

She reached the gate safely and out into the street. At first she kept to the back streets and side alleys, but at last she risked joining a main road, and was rewarded by the sight of a passing cab. She gave the cabbie the address of the Baines's house, climbed in and sank back against the squabs.

Luckily butchers rise early and the first lights were coming on as she arrived. A smiling Mr. Baines called his wife and Alice came flying down the stairs to greet her.

"Now you have come to stay with us," she said joyfully.

"Oh, no, Alice dear. I might put you in danger. Just

let me hide here for a day and tomorrow I will just slip away."

"But where will you go?" Alice wailed.

"To Brighton."

"You cannot return to your house. It is the first place that man will look for you."

Cecilia raised her head proudly and her eyes gleamed with determination.

"Not the house," she replied. "I have just remembered somewhere else, where I will be perfectly safe. Please do not worry about me. I am going to *Paradise*."

CHAPTER TWO

For the last stretch of the journey over the Milton estate, the sun had vanished behind dark clouds, casting a gloomy shadow over the land, in keeping with the Earl's mood.

When at last the carriage drew up outside the great house, John, the Earl Milton, climbed out and walked straight through the door that a footman was holding open for him. He strode through the hall and down the passage to his smoking room. Anyone, looking at his face, would have known that he was angry.

He walked to the window to stare almost blindly at the flowers which were growing in the garden beneath him.

"Two years," he muttered bitterly. "Two years of working to bring this place back to its glory, only to be told that I am almost penniless. All right, I spent more than I intended, but the result is marvellous."

Even so, the meeting with his lawyers had brought him down to earth with a bump. He owned a great estate but no money for its upkeep.

For a moment he almost wished he was back with his regiment fighting in the Crimea. It had been a dreadful war, but life had then held a simplicity that appealed to him now.

In the Barrack hospital at Scutari he had contracted cholera, and for days his life had hung in the balance. At last the devoted care of Miss Florence Nightingale and her nurses had drawn him back from the brink and he had awakened to a new world.

He was painfully thin and exhausted. He felt a strange sense of not knowing who or where he was, although, if asked, he could have recited his name and regiment. But everything in the universe was now different. And so was he.

From the hospital he had been sent directly home, summoned by a telegram that proclaimed his brother had died.

He sailed for England, still afflicted by the eerie sense of having one foot in this world and one in the next and of belonging in neither. The telegram had given no details of his brother's death.

It had been a hunting accident, he learned on arriving home. Now he was the heir to the Earldom. It did not seem real. Nothing did.

John had found his father haggard and distraught. He had lived for his elder son. Now he looked his younger son up and down, sighed and said, "at least you returned safely. It will all be yours now."

He had started to say that he did not want any inheritance at such a price, but his voice had faltered before the bleakness in his father's eyes. Lord Milton was not interested in anything John had to say. He had waited to see him arrive home, for the sake of the estate. After that it was finished for him.

That night he took his own life.

John had been left stunned by this act of abandonment. He found himself sole heir to a property that was in a bad state of repair. He was determined to restore it to its old magnificence, partly for love of the place, and partly to fill the aching void within himself.

For the last two years he had seldom left his estate. Once he had enjoyed London society. Now it seemed to him all noise and meaningless bustle, especially since everyone wanted to discuss the war in the Crimea.

Thanks to an intrepid correspondent for *The Times*, this war had been brought home to the public far more than any previous war. He had described the suffering of the soldiers, the heroism of Miss Nightingale and the folly of the commanding officers.

That folly had been largely to blame for the action where John had received the wound that almost killed him. The supreme stupidity of charging the Russian guns had filled the British public with horror. It had become known as the *Charge of the Light Brigade* and the survivors were lauded as heroes.

A new medal had been devised known as the Victoria Cross. The previous year John and sixty-one other men had gathered in Hyde Park, in London, where the young Queen, mounted on horseback, had personally pinned the decoration on each man.

Somehow John had survived the festivities, but he had no wish to be reminded of something that still filled him with horror and soon he had escaped to his estate.

There he had buried himself in the task of restoring his home, too absorbed to notice that money was running dangerously low.

Now the estate was greatly improved. But it had taken every penny, and there was still much to be done.

'What I need is a miracle,' he thought to himself. 'but where is one to be found?'

The butler entered the room.

"There is a very rich lady to see you, my Lord."

John looked at him, puzzled.

"That's a very odd introduction, Carter. How do you know she is rich?"

"Everyone knows about Mrs. Dilney's money, my Lord. She is famous for it."

"I see. Then perhaps you had better show her in."

As soon as the woman entered John realised that there was no doubt as to her wealth. She was wearing a coat of the finest fur. There were diamonds shining in her ears and also on the fingers of the hand she held out to him.

"Good morning, Lord Milton," she gushed. "I am Anthea Dilney and I am delighted to meet you."

He murmured something polite. He did not realise that one of the reasons for her delight was that he was an exceedingly good-looking young man.

"I have been hoping for some time that our paths would cross," Mrs. Dilney began.

"I am afraid I haven't been around much in society," John said.

"Then you will not have heard of me," she declared, clearly implying that nothing else could account for such a remarkable oversight.

"I am American," she continued, "although my mother was English. She reared me to value her country as much as my father's and I have always wanted to live here for a while. So that is what I plan to do, hire a real old English country estate and enjoy being a great lady."

John mumbled something polite. He was too stunned to think of anything meaningful to say.

"I have been searching for a house as magnificent as this one. I think that your garden and the estate, until you neglected it, must have been very beautiful."

John drew in his breath before replying,

"It has, I admit, been neglected. I have done my best

to put it right, but the work is still far from complete."

"Nonetheless I would like to rent this house from you."

For a moment it was impossible for him to speak, he was so surprised. Then he said,

"I would be only too glad, but you do realise that so much remains to be done."

"Then I shall do it. My dear father left me enough money to do as I please and it will amuse me to undertake some of the work here."

He stared at her in astonishment.

"Are you saying, madam, that you would like to rent the estate as it is?"

"I want to rent it and repair it. It will be fun."

"For how long?"

"For three or four years," she replied, "then I will be returning to America. But for the moment I have a great longing to be an English lady."

Although he could hardly believe it, she was completely serious. Feeling dazed by the speed of events, John arranged for her to meet his man of business the next day.

When he was alone that night he said to himself,

'This is a miracle from Heaven itself and I will go down on my knees in gratitude.'

Then he told himself he was perhaps asking too much, even of God. As an ordinary man with very big debts, he had to be so careful at what was happening that it would be wrong to ask for more.

But an even bigger surprise was waiting for him.

*

Mrs. Dilney returned next day and signed an

agreement to rent the whole Milton estate at the largest sum John dared to ask. She would take possession at the end of the month.

'All I have to do now,' he thought, while wandering in the garden, 'is to find myself another home and a way of filling my time so that I do not brood on how empty my life is. I suppose I am an ungrateful dog to feel like this when I have so much.'

But he knew that he possessed very little that mattered. There was no warmth or affection in his life. He knew many women who would gladly have married him for his title, some of them wealthy. But how many of them would marry him for love?

He could not have answered that question. All he knew was that he had never found the special girl who could have made him want to win her heart.

He realised that he was still lost in the troubled dream that had afflicted him ever since he had gone to the Crimea. Now he looked back on that time with bewilderment, wondering how he could ever have thought there was excitement to be found in war.

For a time he had found peace in renovating the estate. But now he would need something else to give purpose to his life and he could not imagine what it might be.

Strolling back to the house, he became aware that Carter was calling to him in some agitation.

"There is a person to see you, my Lord. A male person."

"Does he have a name?"

"He said to tell you that Sergeant Dale is here and he added, 'if it's him, he'll know me.'"

"Sergeant Dale?" John shouted in delight, "by all that's wonderful! Robert!"

He hurried into the house and found his old comrade standing in the hall. Robert turned his beaming, good-humoured face to him, and they clasped each other's hands.

"It is so good to see your Lordship alive and well," Robert exclaimed. I had almost given up hope when I heard a rumour that you had lived to become the Earl. It seemed too good to be true."

"It is true all right," John said, signalling to the butler who had followed him in. "Carter, some of the best ale for my friend."

They walked into the library and settled down to a good talk about the old days, raising their ale-filled glasses to each other.

"My brother died and my father chose to follow him," John told him quietly. "Since then I have concentrated on restoring this place but – "

There was something bleak about his shrug that told Robert the whole story.

"Nothing was ever quite the same after the Crimea, was it, sir?" he asked gently.

"No, Robert. Everything that seemed important before – " he shrugged again, then pulled himself together. "What we need are new challenges, but where are they?"

"Well, I have found some new challenges," Robert answered. "When I got home I went into the business with my father, learning how to be a landlord."

"Do you remember how I used to dream of that?" John replied with a grin. "I still think I might have been good at it."

"I am sure you would, sir. In fact – why didn't I think of it before? *The Paradise*!"

"Is that your ale-house in London?"

"No my Lord, it is my other place. Dad owned a

second house by the sea, left to him by an old friend who had no family. It's not an ale-house but a hotel, catering for quality folk. They are not titled people but they are prosperous. It needs a gentleman to run it. Someone like you."

"Robert, I was only joking. What do I know about running an inn?"

"You kept us in order in the Crimea," Robert said with a grin.

"Tell me about this place. Where is it?"

"Brighton, on the south coast. You know, the place where the Prince Regent built his pavilion. The Town Council bought it from the Queen a few years ago and now it houses exhibitions and concerts. The sea bathing is very popular and since the railway opened people have been flocking to Brighton."

"What is the hotel like?"

"Well, it's not a big one," Robert replied. "It has four double bedrooms and four single and it's right on the sea, overlooking the ocean. Once I had taken over in London, my father came to Brighton to run it himself. He did it up and made it comfortable, but then he died, so now I need someone to run it in his place.

"It has a nice dining room, so there would be money to be made from passing trade as well as guests staying at the hotel."

John was silent for a long moment. Once more he felt as though he was in a dream, but this time the dream was bright and growing brighter by the moment.

"I have no wish to put it into the hands of someone I don't trust, my Lord. And who can I trust better than you?"

"By Jove, I'll do it!" John said suddenly.

It would solve many problems, he realised, including

where he should live while he rented his own property to Mrs. Dilney.

"Stay here tonight, Robert," he urged. "We have a great deal to talk about."

*

The next morning they set off together for London, where they stayed overnight at John's club before taking the train to Brighton the following day. Outside Brighton railway station they found a cab which took them to the *Paradise Hotel*.

John had not been certain what to expect, but he was pleasantly surprised. The building looked like a country house, not grandiose but comfortable. It stood in its own grounds, behind trees that shielded it from the main road.

Before they went inside Robert led him round the back, so that John could see the steps that led down to the beach.

"Do you see the bathing machines?" Robert said, indicating several huts on wheels that stood at the water's edge. "Six of them belong to the hotel. They're booked by the day. Now let's go in."

Inside the hotel John found even more to please him, especially the dining room which overlooked the sea and was full of light from the large windows.

It was well decorated and the furniture looked comfortable. John saw that it could seat twenty people without any difficulty.

On the other side of the dining room the windows looked out over the garden. John noticed that there were flowers blooming in the beds and the tall sturdy trees made a particularly pretty picture.

Robert led John up the stairs to see the eight bedrooms that were served by six bathrooms, all in excellent condition.

John was then shown the kitchen which was clean and very tidy. This was due to Mrs. Jones, the wife of the groom who, Robert assured him was a very good cook.

"Surely you don't do all the cooking yourself," John asked her.

"Oh, no," she replied. "If there are guests staying here, I have help. There are two girls in the village who are very good cooks and we need them if we're full up."

"Are you full often?" John asked.

"In the summer we are," she replied. "And as summer has just started, the crowds are beginning to come to Brighton."

"I have never seen such a marvellous view of the sea," John observed.

"Everyone says that," she said. "The bedrooms with sea views are the most expensive. Now I will prepare your lunch."

As they sat down in the dining room and looked out at the sea, John commented,

"I am surprised that you didn't ask Mr. and Mrs. Jones to take on the *Paradise*."

"Very good people," Robert said. "But I want this place to attract top clientele. And that means someone like yourself to oversee matters."

"Are you proposing to pay me a salary?" John asked with a grin.

"Certainly not, my Lord," Robert said, shocked at the idea of a salaried Earl. "I propose to give you half the profits that you make over the next three months."

Since the summer season was about to start and he was a complete beginner, John knew that this was a good offer.

They continued discussing practical details, but in his heart John was already certain that he had found the mysterious 'something' that he had been looking for.

"But while I am here, I am not an Earl," he declared. "I will be plain John Milton."

"What's the point of being an Earl, if people don't know?" Robert asked, baffled.

"I would like to see how I manage without people being deferential to my title."

"You managed all right in the Crimea, before you even came into your title."

"That was different. I can hardly mount a charge against your guests."

"But if people knew that you were a hero of the Crimea – "

"No," John replied sharply. "That's all over and done with. Never mention it again. I am plain John Milton, and that is final. Let's consider it settled. I will return here in a week, and we will see what sort of landlord I make."

*

John was in a good mood when he and his valet descended from the train at Brighton a week later. This was a new experience and the prospect of being near the sea was invigorating. He had always loved the sea ever since he was a small boy.

He thought it would be a real holiday to be able to swim whenever he wanted.

The air was so much cleaner than it was in London.

When they reached the *Paradise Hotel*, John saw that it was shining in the sunshine.

It looked so bright that he thought he had never received a better welcome than the hotel was giving him at this very moment.

There were flowers at the front of the hotel and even more at the back. When he entered the hall it was to find

Mrs. Jones waiting for him, smiling with delight.

She showed him up to his room where the sun was pouring in through the window.

The Joneses had placed flowers on the dressing table and on the table by his bed.

Frank, his valet, studied the room with approval. He was a good-looking young man, very popular with the female servants at home. But he had been glad to get away from Milton Park, as one of the parlour maids had, as he put it, "started to hear wedding bells where there weren't any." Now he was looking forward to pastures new.

"I have just seen a very pretty kitchen maid – " he commented.

"Behave yourself," John told him, trying to sound stern.

"Yes, my Lord. I would merely like to remark that I think we're both going to be very much at home here."

"Not my Lord," John reminded him. "Mr. Milton."

"Yes, my Lord."

"And don't make yourself too much at home or there will be trouble."

Frank looked crestfallen.

As he walked downstairs, John thought that so far things were going well.

He went into his office and found the book he needed as it would show him how many people had booked tables for luncheon.

He reflected that he would be glad when Miss Campbell arrived. She was a clerk, and skilled in bookkeeping, so Robert had told him.

"She is away at the moment, visiting a sick relative," he had said, "but she should be back any day now. If there are any problems, she will take care of them"

Suddenly there was a knock on the door.

When he said "come in," one of the waiters entered, saying,

"Good morning, Mr. Milton. There is a young lady here and she wishes to book a room."

"Well, that is good news. What do we have available?"

"All the front bedrooms are free, sir."

"Then show her in."

"First I must tell you, sir, that she began by asking for Mr. Dale."

"Robert? He's in London."

"No sir, I think she means old Mr. Dale, the one who died a few months back. She says she met him when she was here before."

"I see. Thank you. I will go and talk to her."

He rose from his desk and was waiting near the window when the door opened and a young woman came into his office.

For a moment John could do nothing but stare. This was the most incredibly lovely girl he had ever seen. Her eyes were large and deep blue, her mouth wide and shapely, her chin firm but elegant. Her hair was golden in the sunshine streaming in through the window.

But her beauty was more than the sum of its charming parts. It had a fragile quality that was like music. He wanted to look at her forever, like a worshipper.

She gave him a shy, tentative smile and he gazed back, lost in wonderment.

"Good morning," she said in a soft, urgent voice.

"Good morning," he said slowly. He was trying to collect his thoughts, but they remained scattered.

"I was hoping that you could find me a room here for a night or two," she said.

"A room?" he echoed vaguely.

"Yes, you do have rooms, don't you?"

"Yes," he replied quickly. "A room. Yes, you would like a room."

He was afraid that he sounded like an idiot. The air was singing in his ears.

"I want somewhere quiet and comfortable," she told him. "Oh, please say you have a room available for me."

"Of course," he answered, pulling himself together with an effort. "It will be delightful to have you. Are you alone or do you have a companion?"

"I am alone," she responded sharply.

Then in a different tone of voice she added,

"As a matter of fact, I do not want anyone to know where I am. So would you be kind enough not to ask my name? If you can find me a room, I can merely be referred to as number One, Two or Three, whichever it is. Then no one need know who I am."

There was a pause. John was rather taken aback. At last he said,

"I hope, although it may seem rude, that you are not running away from the police?"

The young lady laughed.

"No, it's not as bad as that," she said. "I am only running from someone I dislike, and I have no wish to be found."

"I don't really think that calling you One, Two or Three would work very well."

"Then perhaps I could be Miss Smith or some name like that."

"Very well. Miss Smith," John agreed.

"Nobody must know that I am here," she confided urgently. "Truly, I have done nothing wrong. I only want a quiet place to hide. I had hoped that Mr. Dale – but they say he's not here."

"The older Mr. Dale died a few months back. His son now owns the hotel and I work for him. Did you know Mr. Dale well?"

"No, no – I met him only once – I doesn't matter – "

She seemed distracted and frightened.

"I just want a place to hide," she repeated.

"I can certainly provide you with that," John promised.

'It must be a man,' he thought. 'A girl as lovely as this must be pursued by many men. Perhaps she was married. She wore no wedding ring, but then, if she hated her husband, she might have removed it.'

"As you are in hiding, I think you would be wise to sit at a table in the far corner of the dining room," John suggested. "From there you can see everyone entering the room before they see you."

"That is a very good idea," the young lady agreed. "Thank you. And can I have a bedroom overlooking the sea?"

John thought to himself she certainly knew what she wanted.

Then he wondered again what trouble she might be in. She was obviously a lady and well born.

"I will fetch the housekeeper and she will show you the rooms that are available," he said.

"Can I wait behind your desk?" she asked anxiously. "I promise not to look at anything."

"But why – ?"

Then he realised that if anyone came in, she wanted to be able to duck down behind the desk.

"You may do whatever makes you feel safe," he said.

She slipped behind the desk, taking a look out of the window as she did so.

John slipped away, wondering what on earth was happening.

'I wanted a new experience,' he thought, 'and this is certainly new. I have only been here an hour and already I have met a woman of mystery. Whatever will the next thing be?'

CHAPTER THREE

Cecilia waited while Mrs. Jones was summoned from the kitchen to show her up to her room. She was badly disconcerted and needed a few moments to get her breath back.

She had counted on finding old Mr. Dale, a man who had once been kind to her and she was sure would have remembered her. But now he was dead and his son was not here. There was only the young man she had met downstairs and he was the manager of the *Paradise Hotel*.

She had to admit that he was pleasant and helpful. He had allowed her to remain, despite her suspicious lack of a maid. All was not yet lost.

He was good-looking too, she reflected – tall and upright, with the air of a soldier rather than an hotelier. And his face was so handsome that he might well have been the Knight in shining armour she had once dreamed of meeting.

'But, of course, if I had, Papa would have sent him away because he doesn't have a title,' she thought. 'He would not be impressed by his warm voice and twinkling eyes. And perhaps I shouldn't be, either. I have to think only of my escape. I cannot let myself be distracted, even by the most handsome man I have ever seen.'

Upstairs she studied the room that Mrs. Jones was showing her, and liked it. It overlooked the sea and the sight of the sun dancing on the water made her feel more cheerful.

After Cecilia had walked downstairs, she informed the handsome young hotel manager that she would like to take the room for a week.

"It's room No. 7, sir," Mrs. Jones added.

"I will write it in the book," John said. "Miss Smith, I am glad you have found something that suits you. I do hope you will be happy here."

"I know I will be," she enthused fervently. "Thank you, thank you for being so kind and understanding. I will go up now and unpack. Then I am going to rest for a while, as I have been awake all night."

She could sense their surprise that a young lady so elegantly dressed should be doing her own unpacking.

"Will your maid be following soon, miss?" Mrs. Jones asked.

"My maid?" Cecilia echoed, thinking quickly. "No – er – I had to leave her behind – that is, she has a sick aunt and had to visit her."

"That will be all, thank you, Mrs. Jones," John said hurriedly.

The older woman gave him a strange look and departed for the kitchen.

"We should have thought of that," John said. "Questions are bound to be asked. Do you wish me to arrange for one of our maids to help you?"

"Oh, no, thank you, but the fewer people who see me the better," Cecilia informed him quickly. "But how nice of you to think of ways to help me. I will try not to cause you any trouble."

"I am delighted to do all I can for you," John replied with a little bow.

"I will go now and stay out of sight."

He watched as she returned upstairs and it was only then that he realised that his words were the truth. There was something about her that seemed to draw him and make him want to defend and protect her.

He wondered if he could ask her to explain to him what was frightening her.

Then he told himself it was not his business to ask questions which she would not want to answer. He sat down again at his desk and smiled ruefully.

'We live and learn,' he said to himself. 'I suppose sooner or later she will tell me what this is all about.'

Then he sighed.

'She is certainly one of the loveliest girls I have seen for a long time,' he mused. 'And one of the most intriguing. Now, how do I enter her booking?'

He opened various ledgers, trying to make head or tail of their mysteries.

"May I ask just what you think you are doing?" came an indignant voice from the door.

He looked up to see another young woman standing there. She was about the same age as Miss Smith, but that was all they had in common. This one had a plain face and sandy hair, drawn back severely against her forehead.

"Nobody is allowed to look at those books," she said furiously, advancing into the room. "They are strictly confidential."

"I am glad to hear it, or our customers would have something to complain about," John said.

"*Our* customers?"

"You must be Miss Campbell. At least, I hope you are."

"You are correct. I am she," she announced in a voice

38

that John afterwards described as being like the crack of doom.

"Ah," he said, rising with relief. "I am John Milton, whom Robert has engaged as his manager. He told me about you. He said you know everything about how this establishment works and will be able to explain all the books."

"Certainly," she replied in a brisk tone. "Although my opinion is that it would be better if you left the books entirely to me."

"But isn't that what I am supposed to be here for?" he asked.

She eyed him ironically.

"Very well," she said. "I will explain everything to you and you can take over at once."

Something about the way she spoke struck him as ominous.

"We have a new guest in No. 7," he explained, "and I was trying to find out where to make the correct entry."

"Here," Miss Campbell said, pulling out a ledger he had not noticed before. "This column is for the date, this one for the room number. Here is where you enter the name and home address."

She sat down with the ledger open before her and a pen in her hand.

"Name?" she enquired.

"Miss Smith."

She looked at him quizzically.

"Her first name?"

"I didn't ask."

"Where does she come from?"

"I didn't ask that either."

"I see," she said knowingly.

"What does that mean?"

"She cannot stay here. This is a respectable hotel."

"And she is a respectable young lady," John retorted crossly.

"She is called Miss Smith and she comes from nowhere," Miss Campbell asserted sceptically. "Sir, let me tell you something. There are a thousand Miss Smiths with no addresses swarming all over decent hotels and wise managers get rid of them quickly."

John was suddenly very angry.

"Miss Campbell, if you are suggesting what I think you are, the notion is monstrous and I require you to say no more."

She gave him a shrewd look.

"She must be very pretty," she observed ironically.

"I resent that suggestion."

"You mean she's not pretty?"

"I mean that I will not be interrogated by my staff," he said, feeling harassed.

"In that case," she said coolly, "let us get back to work."

She returned to the books and took him through them with an assurance that soon made him realise that he was at a hopeless disadvantage. As a soldier he had been known for his logical and organised mind, but as a hotel keeper he was no match for this martinet.

"Yes," he said at last. "Well, perhaps if I leave matters in your hands for a while – "

"That would be advisable," she said in an unyielding voice. "I see people beginning to arrive for lunch."

"Then I will get out of your way," he said hastily.

He could see that she was right. People had started coming into the hotel, almost as though someone had waved a magic wand.

By one o'clock the dining room was almost full, Mrs. Jones was very busy in the kitchen, and a pretty waitress in white cap and apron was going round the tables.

As John stood at the dining room door, watching with satisfaction, a wistful voice beside him said,

"That's a sight for sore eyes."

It was Frank, regarding one of the waitresses with yearning.

"Is she the one you mentioned earlier?" John asked, with a grin.

"No, that was the kitchen maid. This is a different girl. Sir, we have really come to the right place."

"Just keep your mind on your job," John ordered. "So that *they* can keep their minds on *their* jobs."

"Yes, sir. Anything you say, sir."

At that moment the pretty waitress glanced up and saw Frank, and the shameless wink he offered her. A knowing smile spread over her face.

"Try not to get us both thrown out," John told his valet.

"We can't be, sir. You are in charge."

"Am I?" he asked grimly.

"You're the master here, sir, the one who must be obeyed, the one before whom we all bow down low."

"Shut up," John told him firmly. He was in no mood for Frank's wit, although on other occasions he would have found it enjoyable.

"Yes, sir," Frank said, suppressing a smile. "Mind you, I don't envy you having to cope with the dragon."

It would have been superfluous to ask who the dragon was.

"How do you know?" John asked.

"I happened to walk past your office."

"Then how can you talk that nonsense about everyone bowing down before me, I cannot imagine. That lady would not bow down before a Russian cavalry charge."

"Yes, she was really flattening you, wasn't she, sir?"

"She was not flattening me, Frank," John said with as much dignity as he could muster. "She was merely instructing me in the fine art of hotel keeping."

"Yes, sir."

"She was also flattening me," John admitted.

Frank grinned.

"Later I am going to turn her loose on you."

Frank's grin faded.

Feeling slightly better, John returned to his office and studied the books, trying to make sense of what Miss Campbell had told him. She had developed methods that were as efficient as they were complex, and an hour's hard work merely served to convince him of the wisdom of leaving the paperwork to her.

More customers arrived. Three of them took rooms in the hotel intending to stay for at least a week. John found that talking to them was most interesting and quite different from anything he had ever experienced. Their mood was always jolly and he found himself being infected by it.

At last he found himself alone, so he decided it would be pleasant to find his way down to the beach. It was a brilliant day and as soon as he stepped out of the hotel he felt the hot sun on his face.

It was a wonderful sensation, peaceful and tranquil. In fact he suddenly felt more like himself than at any time since returning from the Crimea.

The light seemed to flash and dance on the water as he

descended the steps, so that at times he needed to shield his eyes against its radiance. The beach was full of holiday makers, all intent on enjoying the pleasures to be found by the sea.

Lined up at the water's edge were the bathing machines he had noticed earlier. They were huts mounted on wheels. At each end was a door, a flight of steps and harnessing for a horse.

A man or woman entered from the landward side, dressed in everyday clothes and changed inside into a bathing costume. While this was happening, a horse would draw the cabin into the sea, so that the water rose up almost as far as the doors. Then the attendant detached the horse and led it back up the beach.

The bather would then descend a little flight of steps into the water, submerging quickly so that his or her state of comparative undress was seen by as few people as possible. In this way modesty was protected.

When the dip was over the proceedings were reversed. The horse would be attached to the other end of the hut to draw it out of the water and the bather, now once more properly attired, could emerge onto dry land.

That, at any rate, was the theory. But John could see more than one young lady only too happy to flaunt her pretty bathing dress with its short skirt and long legs that came down to her calves, actually exposing her ankles.

The men wore skin tight bathing suits that were even more revealing, with legs that barely reached down as far as their knees, leaving their feet and calves bare. It was the same with the upper part of the suit, which was little more than a vest, revealing bare arms and shoulders. In this way the wearer's manly charms (if he had any) were made manifest to any interested onlookers.

Of course, these costumes were for wearing in the

water. Once on dry land bathers were expected to cover themselves modestly with some kind of robe. But just as the girls were not averse to displaying their pretty shapes in a manner that would have been considered immodest at any other time, so the men also could not resist showing off.

They raced up and down the beach, leaping into the air with yells of glee and occasionally looking over their shoulders to make sure they were being studied by admiring females.

John began to feel definitely overdressed. He wanted to toss aside his confining clothes and run with the sun and wind on his skin. He wanted freedom.

He moved along the beach until he reached the steps that led up to the esplanade. At the top he found himself facing a parade of shops, all dedicated to those who wanted to enjoy life in the sun.

He saw an emporium selling parasols, huge sunshades and beach toys. Next door was a shop full of bathing costumes. There was one male costume and several female. The window was crowded with painted figures, attired in frilly confections, decorated with ribbons and rosebuds. On their heads they wore dainty lace caps, also decorated with ribbons.

John stood gazing at one of these costumes, an enchanting creation in blue, the exact blue of Miss Smith's eyes, he realised. He became aware of a fierce desire to see her wearing it.

It occurred to him that if he wished to bathe he would need a costume. He moved discreetly into the shop and emerged a few minutes later carrying a parcel under his arm. To his own annoyance he could not resist glancing up and down the street in what he was sure was a furtive fashion.

But nobody seemed to be taking any notice of him and he made his escape unnoticed.

He returned to the beach and climbed the steps that led to the *Paradise Hotel*. Half way up he heard a delighted chuckle above his head and looked up to see the enchanting Miss Smith laughing down at him.

"What have you been buying?" she teased. "Share the secret."

"It is hardly a secret."

"But you walk with that parcel as though you had stolen it."

"I most certainly did not steal it."

"Then you are ashamed of buying it."

"I am not," he said defensively. "It is just not the sort of thing that a gentleman wants the whole world to know about."

"Why, what is it?"

"It is a bathing costume, if you must know."

She almost danced with delight.

"Oh, how lovely! I was just thinking how much I would like to go to the beach for a swim."

"Do you think it's safe for you to go down there while it is so crowded?" John asked.

She stopped.

"Oh, I didn't think of that," she answered after a moment. "Perhaps it would be stupid of me to go where I might be seen."

"In fact, it was a little incautious of you to come outside like this," he warned. "Let us go back in, quickly."

John took her arm and they walked into the hotel, shutting themselves in his office.

"Are there definitely people looking for you?" he asked. "No one has come here making enquiries for a missing lady. You seem safe for the moment."

"Perhaps I am. But you are right about going out. I will wait until it's dark or maybe early tomorrow morning."

"I think tomorrow morning would be most sensible," he replied. "After all, at night you might get lost and swept away in the night and however hard we tried, we wouldn't be able to find you."

"Would you really come to look for me?" she asked.

He suppressed a desire to say that now he had met her, he would search for her unto the ends of the earth, and forced himself to say simply,

"Of course I would. While you are here I am your protector and adviser."

Miss Smith laughed.

She was so charming that John found his head spinning even faster.

He wondered again what she could have done to make someone chase after her.

"Is it safe for me," she enquired after a moment, "to come down to dinner?"

"You may have dinner served in your room if you prefer."

A teasing impulse made him add,

"If you come down you might find yourself under surveillance by a plain clothes policemen, or anyone else from whom you are hiding."

"I am not hiding from the police," she stated firmly. "That is one thing you can be sure about."

"I am sorry," John said, meaning it. "I was just trying to be humorous, but whatever this is all about, it isn't funny to you, is it?"

"No," she said with a touch of sadness. "It is not."

"Will you not tell me?" he asked gently.

"Perhaps, one day. But not now."

"You are afraid you cannot trust me, aren't you?"

She gazed at him with a strange, wistful look on her face.

"I think I can but – please, give me a little time."

"All the time you need," John said gently.

"I think I will return to my room," she said, "and perhaps read a book until it is time for dinner. Only – oh, dear! I didn't bring any books with me. I left in such a hurry – "

She checked herself suddenly, as though afraid she was saying too much.

"You can have this one of mine," he said, reaching into a bag by the desk. "Only, I am not sure that it would interest a lady. It describes in detail how we conquered India and how important that country is to us at the moment."

To his surprise, she gave a cry.

"I would love that," she said. "My father was in India at one time and I always hoped he would take me there."

It was true. Much of her Papa's wealth had been built on Indian merchandise, especially textiles.

"I will take great care of it," she promised, taking the book, "and thank you very much for your help."

Holding the book about India in her hand, she slipped out of the office and ran up the stairs, leaving John standing there, puzzled and intrigued.

Who on earth could she be and what was the mystery surrounding her?

Could she really be a woman of ill-repute as Miss Campbell had implied?

But his mind resisted that thought as monstrous. This woman was a lady. She possessed elegance and refinement and a great beauty that came from within, the product of a true and honest soul.

Then he asked himself how he could be certain. They had met only that very day and he did not know her.

In the same breath he was convinced that he did know her and that he had always known her in his heart. And he always would.

It was a moment of revelation that stunned him.

He did not even know her real name. But he knew *her*. And that knowledge would determine all the rest of his life.

He sat down, trying to come to terms with what was happening to him. It was very difficult and at last he pushed the thought away, as though it was something he feared – and perhaps he did.

To give himself something else to think about, he settled down to study the hotel's books, determined not to allow the fearsome Miss Campbell to catch him on the wrong foot again.

He managed reasonably well for a couple of hours before several young men arrived and asked if there was somewhere they could change into their bathing clothes.

John had already discovered that six of the bathing machines on the beach belonged to the hotel and three remained unbooked.

These were immediately taken by the newcomers, one of whom then leaned across the desk and asked in a conspiratorial voice,

"Do you have a shop here where we can buy – " he lowered his voice still further, and almost mouthed the last words, "bathing costumes?"

He looked around furtively as he spoke, as though fearful of being overheard making such a shocking suggestion.

"I am afraid not," John replied. "But there is a shop on the esplanade."

He mentioned the shop's name. The gentleman thanked him and hurried away, leaving John very thoughtful.

The query had given him an idea, but he needed more time to work out the details.

By three o'clock there was very little left to do and he was just wondering if he would go down to the sea again, when he heard a large carriage arrive outside.

A few minutes later a man came into the office. He seemed to be someone of importance, or at least who considered himself someone of importance.

He was middle-aged with a heavy body and broad shoulders. His hair was grey and thinning, his face red and ill-tempered and his expression showed that he would expect to receive what he wanted immediately, with no difficulty about it.

A strange feeling came over John. He could not have explained his thoughts, but he was suddenly convinced that this unpleasant looking stranger had come in search of Miss Smith.

And that her danger was very real.

CHAPTER FOUR

"Good afternoon sir," said John, rising to his feet.

The stranger's response was to glare at him as though the greeting was a form of impertinence. He seemed to bristle, giving the impression that nobody should speak to him without being spoken to first.

And then he demanded,

"Where is the owner of this place?"

"He is not here," John informed him. "I am the manager."

"I want to see the owner. Old fellow. Name of Dale."

Now John knew that this was the man Miss Smith was fleeing. She too had asked for old Mr. Dale.

"Unfortunately Mr. Dale is no longer with us," he said.

"Then where is he?" the man bawled. "That is what I want to know. Are you stupid?"

"I hope not sir. I meant only that Mr. Dale is dead. His son now owns this hotel and he is in London. As I am the manager, I am at your disposal."

"Very well, my good fellow, I have some questions to ask you, and you had better answer them truthfully, or it will be the worse for you."

Nobody had spoken to John in such a manner since he had been a young boy at school and his temper rose.

"I am not in the habit of telling lies," he snapped, "or of allowing people to call me a liar."

"Now, you listen to me," the intruder replied, his colour rising, "I will not stand for being answered back by a servant. You will answer my questions, and then you will keep quiet and listen."

John controlled his temper, annoyed at himself for letting it get the better of him. He had come to this place of his own free will, choosing to discard his title, so that he could enjoy playing at being an inn-keeper. How could he complain at being called a servant?

But to be called a servant by this obnoxious creature was another matter. He was overdressed with an attempt at luxury that did not convince, partly because of the gravy stains down his waistcoat. His coat might once have been costly, but it was no longer in fashion and the cuffs were fraying. A strong whiff of cheap cologne arose from him, not quite disguising the fact that he had not washed recently.

But it was not merely physical revulsion that seized John. There was something about this man, with his mean little eyes and the vicious twist to his mouth that sickened his spirit. Nevertheless, he resolved to be cautious and let the man think him dull witted.

"Yes, sir," he offered in a suddenly meek voice. "How can I help you?"

"That's better. I am looking for a young lady who may have come here."

John was instantly alert, his thoughts flying to the lovely, vulnerable girl in her room upstairs. But he concealed his inward tension by staring at the man as stupidly as he could manage.

"Lots of young ladies come here, sir," he said, speaking slowly. "With their families of course, because this is a very respectable hotel. They come for the sea bathing."

51

In a burst of apparent inspiration, he added, "it's very healthy, you know, sea bathing."

"Yes, yes, I am sure it is," the man responded impatiently. "I don't need a lecture from you."

"I was only trying to be helpful, sir," John said with an air of injured innocence. *"You* said you were looking for a young lady, and *I* said – "

"I know what I said," came the snappish reply. "This is a very particular young lady. You would notice her because she is alone, with no maid – "

"Then she isn't here," John said at once. "We don't admit that sort of young lady."

"What do you mean 'that sort'?"

Remembering Miss Campbell's strictures, John contrived to look bashful.

"You know – *that sort.* This is a respectable hotel."

"It is also small and concealed from the road. Just the kind of place where she would try to hide."

John frowned, apparently making a huge effort of concentration.

"But how could she hide from you, sir? You are here."

"Exactly. I knew where to search for her and now I demand that you take me to her."

"Take you to whom, sir?"

The man drew an exasperated breath.

"To the young lady who came here."

"But she did not, sir. This is a respectable hotel – "

"If you say that once more – " The man checked himself with a sharp breath that sounded like a hiss.

"This young lady is someone of importance," he resumed, speaking with difficulty. "Her family would pay well to recover her."

John's loathing of this creature was overwhelming and almost choked him. For a moment he could not think straight, and forced himself to look down at the visitors book lying in front of him, to conceal his expression.

He felt as though he was crossing a tightrope. The pretence of idiocy was not easy to maintain. But then the irascible stranger was himself none too intelligent, or he might have noticed the contrast between John's present dull vagueness and the resolute spirit with which he had spoken at first.

John decided that this man held a poor opinion of everyone else. In his own mind he was the centre of the world, which made him a fool who could be duped.

And John was going to dupe him, because an inner voice was whispering that this meeting was the most important of his life, and great things might depend on it.

The man was becoming impatient, tapping his fingers on the desk. At last John said,

"Did you say a young lady?"

"Yes I did. I thought we settled that some minutes ago."

John looked up at him, his expression blank.

"Settled what, sir?"

"That she is a young lady and that she is here."

"She is not here, sir. We have to be careful because this is a respect – "

He fell silent before the awful retribution in the other man's eyes.

"She is young, attractive and well-dressed," the stranger continued stormily. "And travelling alone!"

"I cannot think of anyone at the moment who is here alone for luncheon," John said. "Of course someone might have walked into the dining room without my seeing."

"I looked in the dining room on my way in," he replied sharply. "There were only two people and they were old."

"Perhaps the young lady has gone straight to the beach," John suggested.

"Hardly likely. And surely, if she came here alone, you would have noticed her and expected her to book a room. Or perhaps she might ask to use one of the bathing machines, which I understand the hotel owns."

"They are often used without being reserved," John told him as if making a melancholy comment on the perfidy of the human race.

In truth he had not the faintest idea whether what he had said was true or not. He was saying anything that came into his head in an attempt to drive this creature out of the hotel.

"Perhaps you should go down to the beach," John continued. "Look at the bathing machines and see for yourself if they are being used by someone who has not made a proper reservation."

There was silence while it was obvious the intruder was thinking this over. At last he snapped,

"This is nonsense. She would hardly go bathing, at least, not so soon. She would have other things on her mind."

"What other things, sir?"

"She's running away."

"From you, sir?"

"Yes, damn your impudence! I am her lawful guardian. I have total authority over that young woman, and anyone who hides her from me will face a heavy penalty. Do I make myself clear?"

"Yes, sir," John said woodenly. Inwardly he was vowing not to give her up to this man, no matter what the penalties.

After glaring for a moment, the vulgarian, seeming to realise that he was getting nowhere, turned and stalked out, slamming the door behind him. John saw him walk towards the steps which led to the beach below.

As soon as he was out of sight, John hurried up the stairs and knocked on the door of Miss Smith's room.

There was silence for a moment before she called, in a rather frightened voice,

"Come in."

He opened the door and saw at once how relieved she was to see him and no one else.

He slipped quickly inside and shut the door behind him.

"A man has just been here asking about you."

She gave a cry of horror.

"Oh, no, I was so afraid of this."

"I have told him you are not here in the hotel and he has gone down to the beach to see if you are bathing."

"Oh, please, he must not find me."

"There is no reason why he should. When he returns from searching the beach, I will think of something to get rid of him."

"Thank you very much, you have been so kind," Miss Smith said. "Whatever happens he must not find me. Please, please, he *mustn't.*"

He began to realise that she was not merely frightened, but terrified.

"When I leave, you must lock your door and don't open it on any account," he advised. "I will let you know when he has finally gone."

She drew in her breath.

"You are so kind," she sighed. "What would I do without your help?"

"You don't have to do without my help," he answered gently. "I will not let him find you."

She gasped and for a moment he thought she would burst into tears. He longed to beg her to tell him everything, but he could see the fear in her eyes, and he knew it would be a mistake to risk making things worse than they were already.

"Suppose he insists on searching the hotel?" she asked in a shaking voice. "Perhaps I could hide in the attic or the cellar."

"You must stay here," he said firmly. "I won't let him near this room. I will go downstairs and hide my visitors book, and tell the staff not to answer any questions he might ask them."

"Please, please do that for me," she breathed.

He hurried down the stairs to his office, where he locked the visitors book away. Then he went to inspect the taproom which, he was pleased to notice, was doing a brisk business.

Frank was ahead of him, standing behind the bar, receiving instructions in wines, beers and spirits from an enchanting red-haired barmaid.

"Keeping busy, Frank?" John asked amiably.

"Just wanting to do my bit, sir. I believe the hotel is a little short-staffed, and if you should want me to take a turn behind the bar – ?"

"You would be only too delighted."

"I believe I'd be up to the task sir, after this young lady's excellent instructions."

"And this young lady is – ?"

"Ellie, sir," the girl said with a little bob.

Frank gave her a little nudge.

"I am really good at this, aren't I, Ellie?" Frank urged.

Ellie giggled.

"Do you work here all day?" John asked her.

"Oh, no, sir. I usually take an hour off about now."

"Good. Then off you go. Frank will stay here and show me what you have taught him."

Ellie vanished. Frank looked aggrieved.

"Things were just going very nicely here, sir."

"Until I came along and spoiled it. Never mind, you will have other chances. Pour us both some ale and then I want you to go round everyone who works here telling them not to answer any questions about our guests – from anyone."

"You mean if that ugly fellow with the red face comes back?" Frank asked shrewdly, pouring ale into two glasses.

John did not ask how Frank knew about the visitor. Frank had a habit of being everywhere and knowing everything. It made him invaluable.

"Exactly," he said. "I hope we won't see him again but just in case – "

"But isn't that him over there?" Frank asked, pointing.

John groaned as he saw that the ill-tempered stranger had just come through the front door and was making his way to the office. John saw him rattle on the door, scowling angrily and then head for the taproom.

John busied himself serving some customers, forcing him to wait, which did not improve his temper.

"There you are," he barked when he reached the front of the queue. "I've had a fruitless search, thanks to you. The man in charge of the bathing huts says she has not been there."

"Oh, dear," John said, raising his glass for a welcome sip of ale.

Scowling the man snatched up Frank's glass, which

Frank had been about to lift.

"Let me see if your ale is any better than your information," he snapped.

"Our ale is world famous," John informed him, without the slightest basis for such an assertion.

"Yes, everyone likes to try our ale," Frank declared, adding under his breath, "including me."

The man drained the glass and shoved it across the counter.

"It's not bad," he said. "I'll have another one."

He stared at Frank, who was regarding him with horror.

"You! Don't stand there staring at me like a halfwit. Fill up my glass."

"I will do it," John answered quickly. He had the gravest fears about what his enraged valet might put into the ale. "Be off, Frank."

Still glaring, Frank slipped away. John pushed the full glass back across the counter.

"Are you certain she's not here?" the man demanded. "Perhaps I should visit the bedrooms."

"I am afraid you cannot do that, sir," John declared at once.

"Who are you to tell me what I can and cannot do? Do you know who I am?"

"No, sir, but I know who you are not. You are not my employer. He pays my wages and gives me orders, and he would skin me alive if I let you insult guests in this hotel with questions as to who they are and who they have seen."

"He doesn't have to know, damn you!"

"I am sorry but I owe him my loyalty."

"Oh, loyalty is it?" was the sneering reply. "Here

then." He took out a gold coin and laid it down between them.

"What's that?" John said, looking at it.

"That is a sovereign. It is the price of your so-called loyalty and probably ten times what it's worth."

"But my loyalty is not for sale," John replied quietly.

"Oh, be damned to you for a thieving knave! All right, all right. Two guineas!"

John picked them both up and studied them. Out of the corner of his eye he could just see Frank, half hidden around the corner, watching everything.

"Three would be better," he said at last.

Swearing vilely the man pulled out a third guinea and slammed it down.

"Now then," he growled.

"Now then what, sir?"

"Take me upstairs and then disappear."

"I could not do that, sir. My employer would not like it."

The man's face assumed an alarming colour.

"Now look here – " he howled.

Smiling, John raised his hand holding the coins and let them fall from his palm, straight into the man's full glass of ale, causing it to slop over the side.

"Look what you're doing!" the man bawled, dabbing at his waistcoat.

"I am very sorry, sir," John said apologetically. "I cannot think how I came to do that."

"*Clumsy oaf!*"

"Yes sir, but look at it this way. At least you now have your money back."

The man eyed him balefully. Then he seized his glass

and drank the liquid, just as it was, complete with grubby coins, which he retrieved at the last minute. John made a face of disgust and just caught sight of Frank doing the same.

"Look here, I have to find her and that's that."

"You must take my word for it that she is not here," John insisted. "There are many other hotels in Brighton. She could be at any one of them. Of course, if she turns up, I could tell her your name, if you would give it to me, and inform her that she is being sought."

"That would only make her go further afield, perhaps to London."

John made an expressive gesture with his hands before he said,

"I am sorry, but I cannot help you."

"I may come back later to see for myself. But if you do see her, tell her that she must return home immediately. If she doesn't it could be to her disadvantage to remain here or anywhere else."

He spoke the words loudly and disagreeably, and his voice rang out through the taproom.

"I will certainly pass on your message, if I should see her," John said, "but what name shall I tell her?"

The man looked at him as though regarding a worm before drawing himself up to his full height.

"My name," he announced loftily, "is Sir Stewart Paxton. Have you got that? *Sir* Stewart Paxton."

"Sir Stewart," John repeated, apparently awed. "Fancy that! A real Lord."

"That's right. I don't suppose you get many Lords in this place."

"Don't reckon I ever saw one before," John responded humbly. "Are you a very great Lord?"

"Very great," declared Sir Stewart. "I sit in the House

of Lords in London, and help to pass the laws of this country. So now do you understand why you must do as I tell you and give me all the help I require?"

"Oh, yes, sir." John tried to sound impressed.

"So what have you got to tell me?"

"About what, sir?"

"About the missing lady?"

"But there is no missing lady here, sir."

Sir Stewart drew in a long, slow breath, then let it out again just as slowly.

"I will be back," he said at last. "Do you understand that? I will be back!"

He left, slamming the door behind him.

"Yes, I am afraid you will," John sighed.

Frank reappeared.

"Why didn't you slaughter him, sir?" he wanted to know. "Why didn't you take a sword and run it through his gullet?"

"First, because I don't have a sword and second, because to put an end to his miserable life, while possibly justified and even perhaps a service to humanity, might attract unwelcome attention."

"I suppose so." Frank sounded disappointed.

"Pour yourself a fresh glass and get this mess cleaned up."

"Yes, sir. By the way, sir, did he pay for the ale he drank?"

"I never thought of that," John replied guiltily. "I don't think nature designed me for this sort of work."

"I think nature designed you to be an actor, sir. Blowed if I've ever seen a finer performance. How did you know how to act so daft?"

"I learned it from you. It is exactly what you do when I ask you a question you don't find it convenient to answer. You put on a suspiciously innocent, wide-eyed expression – that's it! The one you're doing now."

"I am sure I don't know what you mean, sir. But don't you worry about not being used to the taproom. I am happy to work in here, any time you want."

John grinned and departed, slipping quietly into the hall to see if his unpleasant visitor had left, or was perhaps talking to the servants.

But the man had gone straight out to the yard where a cab was waiting for him. John waited until he had climbed in and departed before running upstairs to tell 'Miss Smith' that she was safe.

He knocked on the door, calling softly,

"It is John Milton here and it is quite safe to let me in."

At once the door opened and she looked up at him fearfully.

"Has he gone? Really and truly?"

"Really and truly."

"Oh, thank goodness!" she cried fervently.

"I wish you had trusted me enough to tell me why you are so frightened of Sir Stewart Paxton, and why you are running away."

He spoke very softly and gently.

There was silence for a moment. Then Miss Smith said, "Perhaps, because you have been so kind and so helpful to me, it is only fair I should tell you what I am doing."

"You don't have to tell me, but I really would like to know what this is all about. And, of course, the more I know about your enemy, the better chance I will have to defeat him."

She laughed and it struck him as a delightful sound.

"How cleverly you put it," she said. "I will of course tell you everything."

John sat down on a chair beside the bed and prepared to listen.

"I had to flee Sir Stewart because I was not strong enough to keep on fighting and I was quite certain that, if I had stayed, I might find myself married against my will."

He looked at her in astonishment.

"Married!" he exclaimed. "Is this fellow trying to force you into marrying him?"

"That is exactly what he is trying to do. He is determined to force me up the aisle one way or another."

"But why?" he asked, regarding her with astonishment.

"Because I am rich, very rich," she replied with a sigh. "He has a title but no money, so he needs a rich wife. He was a friend of my father, although I don't think he was a real friend. Papa liked gambling, but he wasn't very good at it. He often played cards with Sir Stewart and lost a lot of money to him.

"I tried to make him see that Sir Stewart was merely making use of him, but I am afraid that dear Papa was rather blinded by the title. He would have loved to have been titled himself and he was more impressed by Sir Stewart than he should have been.

"He used to say that we were honoured to have 'a great man' condescend to us. That used to make me very angry, because I do not think Sir Stewart is a great man at all."

"Neither do I," John agreed with feeling. "He is a vulgar bully. As for his title – a mere Knight. Or is he a Baronet?"

"No, I know he is a Knight, because he used to describe himself as 'a Knight of the Realm' in a very grandiose way."

"Well, that is barely a title at all," John observed, "except, I suppose, to people who don't have one. Just now, when he told me his name, you would have thought he was a Duke or something like that, instead of being the lowliest rank of all. He actually told me that he sits in the House of Lords, which no Knight does. He obviously thinks I am too ignorant to know.

"Mind you, I played up to him, in a way that flattered his vanity. I called him 'a real Lord', sounding as overwhelmed as I could make it, like the stupidest kind of bumpkin."

He spoke without thinking, from the lofty heights of his Earldom, forgetting that she did not know his rank. Then he realised that she was staring at him, bewildered.

"But you do know," she said. "You must have spent a lot of time around aristocrats. In fact, you are more of a gentleman than some people with titles."

"I have met some men of rank in the army, younger sons and so forth," John muttered vaguely.

"You were in the army?" she echoed, delighted. "Oh, how wonderful! Were you in the war in the Crimea?"

"Yes," he replied quietly.

She saw the look on his face and her manner changed.

"Forgive me," she said. "I was thinking of the excitement, but that was stupid of me. It must have been horrible for the men who were actually there."

"It was," he said. "But let us leave it at that."

"Yes," she agreed gently. "We don't have to talk about the war if you would rather not."

Something in her voice made him look up. He saw on her face a look of kindness and understanding and, in some inexplicable way, he felt his heart ease.

CHAPTER FIVE

John felt as though he could have stayed forever, just looking at this wonderful girl with her sweet face. But he forced himself to return to reality. What was he thinking of to be indulging in dreams?

"Perhaps you had better tell me the rest of the story," he suggested. "What did Sir Stewart do?"

"He offered for my hand. Papa was delighted and when I refused he could not believe his ears. We had the most terrible quarrels. He commanded me to say yes and when I wouldn't, he said I was no daughter of his. He called me a disgrace and – oh, many other terrible things.

"I used to overhear him talking to Sir Stewart, promising to 'bring me to my senses' as he put it."

John uttered a bitter oath. It appalled him that this delicate creature should be bullied by two strong men, each of them thinking only of himself and neither caring a rap for her feelings.

It crossed his mind that if she was his to protect, he would never allow even a breath of wind to harm her.

"Papa kept on talking about the wonderful chance I was losing," she continued. "He so badly wanted to be the father-in-law of 'a great Lord' as he called him.

"Then he began saying that he did not feel well and asking me how I could grieve a sick man by my unfilial behaviour. But I still did not give in. I thought it was a trick."

"Which I am sure it was," John observed.

"Wait, let me tell you the rest. Papa sent for his lawyer and made a new will. He told me that he would leave all his money to Sir Stewart, so that I would have to marry him. I said I thought that was an excellent idea, as it would save me from any more of Sir Stewart's pestering."

John guffawed with laughter.

"Good for you," he applauded.

"But then something terrible happened. At that time Papa and I were living in Brighton. Sir Stewart's house is in London, although he spent so much time here that he almost lived with us. But he had returned to London when Papa and I had that last quarrel.

"Papa stormed out of the house, saying he was going to London to tell Sir Stewart about the change of his will. Two days later there came news of a terrible railway accident. The London to Brighton train had been derailed, several carriages had overturned and five people had died."

"Yes, I remember hearing about the tragedy," John said. "The newspapers talked of nothing else for days."

"Papa was one of those who died. He was tossed out of his carriage. And I felt so guilty."

"Why should you?" John demanded. "His so-called 'illness' really was a trick, as you suspected. His death was an accident and nothing to do with you."

"I know but – he used to talk about not being long for this world and then it turned out to be true. Sir Stewart said Papa's dying wish was for our marriage.

"He was with him on the train, you see. He said he held him at the end and Papa said, 'Stewart, protect my darling child. Tell her my last wish is for your marriage.'

Did you say something?"

John had made a violent exclamation.

"What a lot of nonsense!" he said. "It comes straight from a bad novel or a sensational play. I could do better than that myself."

"I must admit it sounded a bit flowery for Papa," she agreed.

"Was this pathetic speech overheard by anyone else?" he demanded ironically.

"It seems not."

"There you are. Sir Stewart invented the whole story."

"But even if Papa didn't actually say it, it was what he wanted. And, but for me, he would not have been on that train – "

"That's enough," John said forcefully. "My dear girl, you have to stop thinking like this. None of it was your fault."

"I tell myself that, yet it just seems so terrible." She flashed John her breath-taking smile. "But I can believe it when you tell me. You make me feel so much better."

"What happened about the will? Did he leave everything to Sir Stewart?"

"No, but he did something worse. He appointed him as my guardian."

"Damn him!" John said softly.

"Sir Stewart forced me to move into his house in London. Since that day he never leaves me in peace. He tells me over and over that Papa's death was my fault, and that I must 'atone' by fulfilling his last wish. He also said that Papa died owing him a lot of money, but he would wipe out the debt if I married him."

"But surely he cannot force you to marry him if you do not want to do so?"

"Oh, it's so easy for a man to say that," Cecilia cried with a touch of exasperation. "But I was a woman alone, in his house and in his power. There was nobody to help me and he is determined to drive me into this marriage by hook or by crook.

"I ran away after eavesdropping and hearing that he was bribing a local parson to help him force me into marriage. Sir Stewart is prepared to go to any lengths, even to drug me so that I would be helpless until it was too late."

"It is the most ghastly story I have ever heard," John exclaimed. "How can any man, who presumably calls himself a gentleman, force a woman into being his wife?"

"He doesn't care what anyone calls him," she said bitterly, "as long as he gets my money. And, as my guardian, he also controls my fortune and he is keeping the purse strings tight in an attempt to force me to give in.

"He dismissed my maid and said I should use a girl from his own house. But she is a slattern and useless as a maid. He just wanted her to spy on me and I often found her in my room going through my belongings.

"That is why I don't have a maid with me. I know it looks strange, but I had to slip away when she wasn't looking."

"I can hardly believe my ears," John said in horror. "How can any man behave like this? Of course you must not be married off by force."

"I suppose it was not very clever of me to come back to Brighton, but it is the only place I know. I still own the house where I lived with Papa, although it's shut up now. I thought I might hide there, but of course I couldn't. It is the first place Sir Stewart would look."

"What made you come here? And how did he know that you might?"

"We all had dinner here one night. Papa tried to

pretend that we were celebrating our engagement. He thought I wouldn't make a scene in public, but I did. They were both furious.

"I got up and ran from the table. Mr. Dale, the landlord was so kind. He told Papa he would throw him out if he didn't stop upsetting me. I thought maybe he was still here, so this was where I came, but I now realise I shouldn't have done.

"I expect Sir Stewart went to the house first, but when I wasn't there he must have remembered this place, and what happened that night."

"He thought Mr. Dale would shelter you," John mused. "And when he found he had died, he was not sure what to think. The longer we can keep him confused the better."

"I have told him again and again that I don't want him to touch me. In fact I would not marry him if he was the only man left in England. There is something so horrid about him that I would rather die than marry him!"

She spoke so violently that John said,

"Now listen, don't upset yourself. I promise you will not be forced into marrying this man."

"But he is so determined," she cried. "You do not know what he is like, how ruthless he can be in getting what he wants. Save me, oh, please save me. I don't know which way to turn."

He could see that she was becoming hysterical. Like most men he was nervous of female hysterics and began to consider escaping. But then something in her wretchedness pierced his heart, and he forgot about himself in his need to comfort her.

"There, there," he said, gathering her into his arms and drawing her close. "There is no need for this. You are safe now, I promise you."

"I don't think I will ever feel safe again in my life," she choked.

John patted her back and she rested her head on his shoulder, a prey to bitter sobs.

"There, there," he said again.

He felt that the words were feeble, but she seemed to find some comfort in them and clung to him.

It felt so sweet to hold her warm, delicate body pressed against his own. A gentle fragrance flowed from her, filling the air, so that John found his head spinning. Gently he stroked her bright hair, feeling its silkiness against his fingers and wondered if he had wandered into Heaven.

"Don't upset yourself," he murmured. "You are with me now and I will not allow anything harmful to happen to you."

"Oh, that sounds so wonderful," she said in a small voice. "If I do marry I want it to be to someone who loves me for myself. Otherwise I would rather stay single."

She looked at him with an expression in her eyes which John found very touching. He thought how dreadful it would be if so much beauty and charm were to be wasted in a spinster life.

"Will you really help me?" she asked softly.

"I promise I will do everything I possibly can," John answered bravely.

She gave a deep sigh which seemed to come from her very heart.

"You have been so clever to send him away empty-handed."

"And that is what I will continue doing if he comes back and tries to find you," John replied kindly. "I think that, for tonight at any rate, you should dine up here in your room. Then if that monster returns he will not be able to find you by looking through the windows."

"Yes, I will stay here," she said purposely. "And I will keep the door locked just in case."

"A good idea. I will ask Mrs. Jones to prepare something special for you and I will carry it up myself."

"And will you stay with me for a while and talk to me, so that I don't get too frightened by myself?"

The idea of being alone with her was so tempting that he took fright. She was so beautiful and so desirable, that he was not sure he could trust himself to behave with propriety.

"I will do my best," he responded, gently disengaging himself from her. "But I have to remember that I am on duty in the hotel and must spend some time looking after the other guests."

"Thank you for being so kind. What would I do without you? Even with your protection I am still very frightened."

"Try not to be," John told her. "We are going to win and when you go into battle, as I found when I was in the army, you have to feel quite certain that you are going to be a better warrior than the man who is up against you. That is what we have to feel at this moment."

He rose to his feet as he finished speaking and said,

"Now I must go back to work because people will be arriving without me present to look after them."

He opened the door before he turned round to say,

"I promise you that you need not be frightened any more. You are safe, completely safe. Perhaps tomorrow we will find another way of winning the battle."

He shut the door before she could answer.

As he walked down the stairs he realised that while she had been talking to him her eyes had been shining.

'What man could resist such eyes?' he thought.

Then he told himself to stop day-dreaming and get on with his work which, after all, was what he was here for.

Downstairs John was pleased to see that the dining room was very busy. He walked through to the kitchen, where Mrs. Jones was deep in her pots and pans.

"The young lady who arrived this afternoon will take supper in her room," he announced. "I want you to prepare her the best menu, and when it's ready – "

He was about to say that she should send for him to carry the tray upstairs when he became aware that Frank was trying to attract his attention.

"We need the key to the cellar," the young man said. "Nobody knows where it is."

"It'll be in your desk," called Mrs. Jones over her shoulder as she plunged into yet another task.

Together John and Frank went searching in his desk until they found the elusive key.

"Have you suddenly appointed yourself part of the catering staff?" John asked as they climbed down the steps to the cellar.

"Well I have to do something to pass the time," his valet replied virtuously. "So I thought I would make myself useful. Hey, look at that!"

He was holding up a lamp so that they could both look around the well-stocked cellar.

"I am going to like this job," Frank exclaimed gleefully.

From somewhere he had obtained a list of the bottles that were needed in the dining room, and they spent a fascinating time seeking them all out before returning upstairs, each of them rather dusty.

They headed for the kitchen where Frank set down the bottles and John checked to see if Miss Smith's supper was ready.

"It has just gone up," Mrs. Jones said.

"Gone up?" he echoed, aghast. "But I was supposed to carry it up myself."

"You didn't say anything about that, sir."

"Yes, I – no, I didn't, did I? Who took it?"

"Miss Campbell. She sometimes helps out when business is brisk."

But John was already halfway up the steps, pursued by Frank, who could see that his master was agitated about something and considered it part of his job to help.

John arrived first to find Miss Smith's door open and a cry coming from inside. She had not put on her light and since darkness was falling rapidly he could not be certain what was happening.

What happened next was too fast for anyone to follow. John dashed into the room to intervene, taking hold of Miss Campbell, who was still holding the tray.

Miss Campbell reacted with a shriek which made Frank also rush into the room, although to do what precisely he could not have said.

"Take your hands off me," Miss Campbell screamed, trying to struggle free of John without dropping the tray.

Somehow Frank, most ill-advisedly, got between them at the precise moment when Miss Campbell started to defend herself. The result was that the soup was spilled all down his trousers and he received a box on his ears that made his eyes water.

Miss Smith lit a lamp and they all stared at each other.

"How dare you!" Miss Campbell howled at Frank in a voice of outrage. "How dare you assault me in that vile manner!"

"It wasn't me," Frank replied indignantly. "It was – "

He started to indicate his employer before realising

that he was in an awkward position.

"It was a misunderstanding," he finished lamely, rubbing his face.

"For which I am to blame," John intervened smoothly. "I intended to bring Miss Smith's supper myself and hurried up to take over from you. But now that we are all here it might be a good moment to explain the situation.

"Miss Smith's presence here is to be concealed and it may be easier to achieve this with the two of you in on the secret. Miss Smith, allow me to introduce my assistant, Frank, and Miss Campbell, who both work at the *Paradise Hotel*."

The two young women stared at each other. Then looks of recognition broke over their faces.

"I remember you," Miss Campbell proclaimed. "You visited the hotel when old Mr. Dale was alive. You were with two men – and there was a terrible row – "

"And you were so kind to me," Miss Smith burst out. "Now I remember you too. I ran away from those men into one of the back rooms and Mr. Dale told you to look after me and you did."

Before the relieved eyes of the men the two girls embraced.

"Thank heavens for that," John said.

"Yes, I thought it was going to turn very nasty for a minute," Frank muttered.

But Miss Campbell evidently had very sharp ears. Breaking from Miss Smith's embrace she turned furiously on Frank.

"It will certainly turn nasty if you dare to manhandle me again," she said firmly. "Very nasty indeed. I trust I make myself quite clear."

"Perfectly," Frank said, rubbing his cheek reminiscently.

"It was not really his fault," John said quickly. "He does not normally go around manhandling young women – "

"Here, I didn't – "

"Silence, Frank," John told him. "I think you should apologise to the young lady."

"Me apologise to her? I am the one that has the soup all down me!"

"Then you had better go and change, hadn't you?" his employer said remorselessly.

"But look at me!"

"Must we?" Miss Campbell asked disdainfully.

"Now see here, miss! You did this and what have you to say about it?"

"Only that it will teach you not to go around manhandling innocent females," she replied with spirit.

"If you say that once more I'll – "

She squared up to him.

"You'll what?"

"I'll – I'll – I'll take offence."

"Fine. Splendid. You've taken offence and I am shaking in my shoes, so now we can consider the matter closed. Don't stand there like a booby with soup all down you. You look ridiculous."

"Suppose I demand that you wash my clothes?"

"Suppose I box your ears again?" she threatened, taking a step towards him.

"Ow, get her off me!" Frank yelped, backing away into the hall. "She's violent."

"Serves you right," John said with a grin, following him out.

"But it wasn't me that manhandled her," Frank said desperately.

"I know, it was me, but I didn't mean to. It was an accident. Come Frank, I am only asking you to save my dignity."

"What's it worth?"

"Let me just say that if you don't keep my secret, I will turn Miss Campbell loose on you with instructions to do her worst."

"You wouldn't!" Frank breathed, awed by this ruthlessness.

"I would. Now go and get changed."

Frank fled.

A moment later Miss Campbell emerged with the ruined supper on the tray and announced that she was going downstairs to fetch another.

"Perhaps, sir, you would be good enough to escort me downstairs," she said loftily. "To protect me from brigands."

"I don't think you need worry," John said in a placating voice. "That particular brigand has gone to change his clothes, but I will be happy to escort you."

As they descended he was profuse in his thanks for the way she was helping out, since it was not her task to be a waitress.

"Old Mr. Dale was always very kind to me," she said. "I would have done anything for him."

In the kitchen John waited while a new supper was set out on the tray and then carried it away himself.

As he passed the dining room he was pleased to see that there were still plenty of customers. The pretty maid who had caught Frank's eye earlier that day was collecting plates and stacking them onto a trolley by the wall.

To John's amusement Frank, evidently having donned clean clothes in a hurry, was also there, talking to her as she worked and generally getting in her way.

"Pretty Cherry," he wheedled. "Such a pretty name for such a pretty girl."

"Who said you could call me Cherry?"

"It is your name, isn't it?"

"It might be and it might not. It is no concern of yours either way."

"But it could be," Frank pleaded.

"Not unless I say so, and I don't say so."

"Is this fellow bothering you?" John asked her. "I can see he is not doing anything useful."

"I am helping," Frank said aggrieved. "I am carrying plates and things."

Cherry regarded him sceptically.

"One plate," she said.

Frank grinned.

"But think how useful I'll be later," he said, "for walking you home."

"I never said you could walk me home," she replied with spirit. "Besides, I only live five minutes away, and I have a friend calling for me."

Frank looked crestfallen.

"A male friend?" he asked.

"Mind your own business, you cheeky boy, and move out of my way."

"Leave her in peace, Frank," John cautioned, drawing him aside. He smiled at Cherry. "Has anyone been here asking questions?"

"Nobody, sir. Do you mean that man who was here earlier? I think he has either found who he wanted or given up the search."

"I only hope you are right," John said.

Over her shoulder he could see Frank making signs,

asking if he should tell Cherry any more than she already knew. He shook his head firmly and set off upstairs.

CHAPTER SIX

John knocked gently on the door of Miss Smith's room, calling,

"It's all right. It is only me."

She opened at once and stood back for him to pass through. She immediately closed the door behind him.

"I am so sorry for the disturbance," he said as he set down the tray on the dressing table. "I hate to think of you being alarmed."

"Don't worry, I am not any more. And it was a relief to find someone that I knew. I like Roseanne so much."

"Roseanne?"

"Yes, that's her name. Did you not know?"

"I met her for the first time this afternoon and she terrifies me."

"She terrifies that poor young man, too," she added, chuckling.

He too began to laugh.

"Poor Frank. He fancies himself as a ladies man, but he's having very bad luck tonight. Roseanne almost knocked him out and Cherry has just snubbed him. Now madam, your supper is served."

He delivered the words with a flourish, drawing out the chair for her and offering her a napkin.

"Thank you, kind sir," she said. "Oh, but what's this?"

He was uncorking a bottle of wine.

"I am sure I did not order wine."

"This is compliments of the house and to celebrate our meeting."

"Oh, yes," she replied eagerly. "I feel so much safer now and that I will always want to celebrate."

John filled two glasses of wine and as they clinked, they both started laughing.

"I am so hungry," she told him, tucking into her supper with gusto. "It has been such a day."

"Do you realise," John said suddenly, "that after all that has happened I still do not know your name? Your first name, I mean."

"Cecilia," she said.

John immediately thought that Cecilia was the prettiest name he had ever heard.

As she ate he began to tell her stories of his life in the army, not the grim tales of war and suffering, but the many light-hearted incidents. She laughed heartily and he began to think that he must be quite a wit.

Somehow the hours slipped by, the most pleasant hours John felt that he had ever spent. But he also felt a little guilty.

"I have been enjoying our conversation so much that I had forgotten I was on duty," he said. "I should really go downstairs and see to – to – "

"See to what?" she asked, smiling as if she perfectly understood his problem.

"See to – whatever needs seeing to," he finished lamely.

"And what would that be?"

"You are not being fair," he protested. "I have admitted to you that I am a novice. I am sure there is something downstairs that I ought to be seeing to."

"If only you knew what it was," she teased. "I expect the guests have finished their dinner and will be playing bridge. And your staff is quite used to running this place without you."

He realised that she did not want him to go and that was a temptation that he knew he must avoid.

"I must leave for your sake," he said. "It isn't proper for me to be here with you alone. I should not really have stayed so long."

"But I trust you," she replied, seeming puzzled.

He was stunned by the innocence in her eyes and her voice. It put him on his honour as a gentleman.

"I have a job to do downstairs," he said firmly, "and it is time I was doing it. Don't forget to lock yourself in when I have gone."

"You have been so kind and so understanding that I am not as frightened as I was when I first arrived," she said fervently.

John smiled at her.

"I want you to go on feeling like that," he asserted. "But you are not to leave this room until I tell you it is safe for you to do so."

He spoke decisively. She nodded.

John gathered up the tray and departed quickly, hurrying down the stairs.

Several of the hotel guests were emerging from the dining room and heading for their rooms. He bid them a courteous goodnight and received compliments for the excellent meal and accommodation.

More guests were coming into the hallway, putting on

their cloaks, ready to leave the hotel.

John looked into the dining room where Cherry was clearing away.

"You have been splendid," he told her, "and I am very grateful to you for all your hard work."

She gave him a charming smile and he knew that his praise had pleased her. Then, because he wanted to do everything properly, he proceeded into the kitchen to say goodnight to Mrs. Jones who was just shutting up for the night. She told him she was tired out and if anyone was still hungry they would have to wait until breakfast.

John laughed.

"It would be wise to leave a little of the excellent cake we enjoyed at teatime and perhaps some of your *petit-fours* on the side table," he said. "Then if anyone arrives late they can help themselves."

"I expect you want to go to bed too," Mrs. Jones said. "It will soon be twelve o'clock."

"But you have been doing the real work," he pointed out with his pleasant smile. "You really are a marvel!"

After saying goodnight to Mrs. Jones, he turned out the lights in the dining room. Then he returned to his office.

Having closed the window he was just making sure he had put all his books away, when he heard someone coming along the passage.

He groaned, afraid that he knew who it was, and sure enough, the next moment Sir Stewart entered his office.

Before he could speak, John said,

"Oh, you are back. I was just shutting up and going to bed."

"I have not yet found the young lady I am looking for," Sir Stewart said. "Are you sure she is not here?"

"I gave you the answer to that question two or three

hours ago," John replied firmly, "and it has not altered."

There was silence for a moment before Sir Stewart asked,

"Are you quite certain you are not hiding this young lady from me? Perhaps she stepped into the hotel while you were busy or maybe having your meal and has disappeared upstairs to find an empty room."

The way he spoke made John afraid he might demanded to examine the hotel for himself.

"I assure you," he replied, "no one has booked a room since you last came here. There have been extra people to dinner, but as you can see the dining room is now closed and they have all left. In fact I am closing the hotel at this very moment."

"Very well, I will take a room for the night," Sir Stewart demanded.

John froze. This was a disaster.

"I am afraid that we are fully booked," he responded stoutly.

"I'm sure you can find something for me."

"And I am sure that we cannot. The hotel is full."

Sir Stewart thrust his hand into pocket and pulled out a handful of gold coins.

"Why don't we get down to business?" he said in an unpleasant, oily voice. "I am sure there's someone you can turn out."

"And I am sure that I have no intention of doing so," John said furiously. "Kindly leave or I shall be forced to send for a policeman."

Sir Stewart drew in his breath sharply.

"Are you drunk to speak to me like that?"

"I can send for a policeman drunk or sober," John pointed out.

Sir Stewart pursed his lips together as if somehow preventing himself from swearing aloud at being thwarted.

After a moment, John said,

"I suggest you give up the chase until tomorrow. I have always found it is impossible to pursue people in the dark. Tomorrow when the sun is shining, it will give you a chance of finding her."

For a moment there was silence. Then Sir Stewart growled.

"Very well, but you haven't heard the last of this."

"There is always another day," John answered, ignoring the threat. "If you take my advice you will look elsewhere. If she is running away from you, I doubt if she will linger where you are likely to be looking for her."

Again there was silence before Sir Stewart replied,

"But if she does turn up, for goodness sake find out where she's going or better still, make her stay here until you can contact me. I am at the *Grand Hotel*."

He saw John looking at him in surprise, and snapped,

"Of course I already have a hotel room. You do not think I would choose to stay in this little place unless I needed to, do you?"

"No, sir," John replied woodenly.

Sir Stewart scribbled his name and the address of the *Grand* on a piece of paper.

"Here," he said, thrusting the paper towards John. "Don't lose it. And make sure all your staff know who they are looking out for."

"Who are we looking out for?" came a voice from behind him.

With shock, John realised that it was Miss Campbell at her most belligerent.

"A young woman," Sir Stewart bawled. "Fair hair, pretty, well-dressed, probably wearing a pink bonnet – "

"Oh, her," said Miss Campbell dismissively.

John could hardly believe his ears. Was this terrifying young woman going to give the game away, after everything she had said?

"You have seen her?" Sir Stewart whirled on John. "You said she wasn't here."

"He never saw her," Miss Campbell replied. "I made sure of that. I have seen her sort before. I get them off the premises before any of the men see them. This is a respectable hotel."

"What do you mean, off the premises?" Sir Stewart demanded.

"I mean out, right out. You cannot take chances with that sort of woman."

"May I ask what you mean by that?" Sir Stewart yelped, briefly diverted by this slur on his intended bride. "Are you implying that she was a woman of bad character?"

"Of course she was. She did not bring a maid. I know what that means. Oh, yes. I told her exactly what she could do and she took herself off."

"When was this?" John asked in a carefully neutral voice.

"About two hours ago, sir. I was going through the books when she came sauntering in, bold as brass, demanding a room. I asked where was her maid and she spun me some daft story about having to leave her behind. No decent woman behaves like that, so I pushed her out of the side door before anyone else could see her."

"Did she say where she was going?" Sir Stewart raged.

"She said something about having to go back to London and give in."

"Give in?" Sir Stewart yelped. "She actually said that?"

"She actually said that. I didn't ask what it meant. I didn't need to. 'Giving in' means just one thing to that sort of woman. I told her London was the best place for her sort."

"London," Sir Stewart breathed.

There was a gleam in his eyes at this hint that he might have won.

John watched him with contempt. Was there no end to this man's stupidity?

"London," Sir Stewart repeated. "And she's given up."

"In," said Miss Campbell firmly.

"What?"

"Not up. In. She's given in. She said so."

"Up or in, it is the same thing."

"Not at all," Miss Campbell said, evidently settling in for an argument. "She definitely said 'give in', and we all know what that means, of course – "

"Don't lecture me, young woman," Sir Stewart howled. "I don't care what it was. I have got her where I want her. Excellent."

Without saying any more, he walked out of the office slamming the door behind him.

John followed him outside and stood watching him climb into his carriage and depart.

He gave a deep sigh of relief.

Sir Stewart Paxton struck him as violent and dangerous and he could understand why Miss Smith would want to flee from him. How could any girl fight such a man?

But she was no longer alone. Now she had a soldier to fight for her and the cunning Miss Campbell. Sir Stewart faced stronger opponents than he realised.

Striding back into the hotel he sought out Miss Campbell.

"Well done!" John congratulated her gleefully. "You were superb!"

"Do you think it worked, sir?"

"Worked? Of course it worked. You did a marvellous job. Frank, did you see her?"

Frank had been hovering. Now he emerged with a grin on his face.

"Yes sir. I felt very sorry for him. He didn't understand the forces he was taking on. Of course," he added thoughtfully, "he was lucky he didn't get his face slapped."

"No, I keep that for men who *particularly* annoy me," Miss Campbell said significantly.

"Ah – yes. I have things to do."

Frank vanished quickly.

Gradually the hotel became dark and silent. The remaining guests had repaired to bed. John noticed Cherry slipping out of a side door with a shadow in determined pursuit.

He heard Frank's voice in gentle persuasion, then the sound of a sharp crack.

"Ow!" sounded his valet's unmistakeable voice.

"You just keep your hands to yourself," came Cherry's voice. "I have told you before."

The side door closed and after a moment Frank emerged through the gloom, rubbing his face. He stopped when he saw his employer and grinned sheepishly.

From the window beside them they could see Cherry walking through the moonlight until she reached the steps down to the beach. Then a man's figure detached itself from the shadows. She gave a cry of delight and ran into his arms.

"Ah, well," Frank sighed philosophically. "I suppose you cannot win every time."

"You don't seem to be winning any of the time," John observed. "Did she hit the same cheek as Miss Campbell?"

"No, sir," Frank said gloomily. "The other one. So now I have a matching pair!"

"You will be safer if you stay away from her, young man," said a voice behind them.

They both turned and saw Miss Campbell.

"I am not afraid of him," Frank asserted, with a touch of defiance.

His tormentor looked him up and down in the gloom, with an expression that showed she was not impressed.

"Well you would be if you had any sense," she pointed out tartly. "The last man who tried to paw Cherry about is still on crutches. Goodnight gentlemen."

She departed without another word.

Frank cleared his throat.

"Well," he said defensively, "I didn't like Cherry *that* much."

"Which is just as well," John noted wryly, "since she doesn't seem to like you at all."

Frank gave him a black look.

John decided to pay a final call on Cecilia, who would sleep better if she knew that Sir Stewart had been fooled into leaving. He locked up his office and made sure that the doors on the ground floor were shut and bolted.

Then he walked up the stairs, knocked on the door of Miss Smith's room and waited for her somewhat frightened voice to ask, "Who is there?"

"It is me, with good news," he replied.

He heard her jump out of bed and run across the floor. She opened the door and stood peeping at him as if to make quite certain it was him and no one else.

"What has happened?" she whispered. "I have been lying here so frightened that he might have forced his way in and was exploring every room in the hotel."

"No, he has gone away. Miss Campbell – Roseanne – invented a clever story about having seen you and driven you off the premises."

"But why would she do that?"

John suddenly became horribly embarrassed and wished he had never started to tell her the story. How could he possibly explain to this delicately reared young lady that she had been called a woman of ill-repute?

"Well – er – it does not matter," he said hastily. "The point is that he now thinks you have gone back to London."

As he was speaking he became aware that she was standing in front of him in her elegant night gown, her long fair hair falling over her shoulders. She looked so enchanting that he was not surprised that she was being chased by a man.

"I am so grateful," she said in a soft voice. "There is no reason for you to be kind to a perfect stranger, but you have been like an angel from Heaven and now I can go to sleep without being frightened."

She gave a deep sigh that touched John's heart.

Then a cough came from the hallway behind him. His blood froze, but when he turned, it was only Miss Campbell, standing there with a thunderous face. Behind her stood Frank, meekly carrying a load of bedding.

"I have decided to sleep here too," she said imperiously. "Miss Smith will be safer."

"But, thanks to you, Sir Stewart has departed," John pointed out.

"Nevertheless, she will be safer," replied Miss Campbell, giving him a gimlet-eyed stare that left no doubt as to which danger she meant.

Then she saw the tray in John's hands, bearing two wine glasses, plus a bottle of the hotel's finest wine and she raised outraged eyes to his face.

"An excellent vintage," she declared frostily.

"Yes, and so thoughtful of him to bring me wine when I hadn't ordered any," Cecilia announced innocently.

"Indeed!" Miss Campbell's face spoke volumes about men who brought wine to a woman's bedroom, unasked.

She moved towards the door, managing to make a stately procession with Frank bringing up the rear.

"All right, my lad," she said. "This is far as you come. Give that to me."

She took the bedding from him, and headed into the room.

"Oh, Roseanne, how kind of you," Cecilia said. She flashed John a smile. "Goodnight."

"Goodnight, Miss Smith."

He barely had time to get the words out before Miss Campbell closed the door firmly in his face.

"She doesn't approve of either of us," Frank observed.

"No, but I am easier in my mind knowing that Miss Smith has such an excellent guardian angel. I am sure Miss Campbell is capable of scaring off all comers."

"Not a doubt of it," Frank observed with feeling. "I have seen bulldogs that scared me less!"

"So have I."

From behind the door they heard Cecilia say,

"Roseanne, do tell me what you said to that horrible man. Why did you 'order me out'?"

John and Frank froze to the spot as a low murmur from Roseanne told them that she was explaining. This was followed by total silence, and then, the very last sound they had expected to hear.

Peal after peal of ringing laughter. Cecilia sounded as though she was almost choking with mirth.

Aghast, the two men stared at each other.

"It just shows you, sir," Frank said. "You cannot tell with females."

"No, you can't," John answered with feeling. "Let's go and have a drink."

*

John rose at six-thirty next morning. Putting on his bathing suit and his coat, he ran down the stairs, out of the door and on to the cliff.

Descending to the beach he was relieved to see that, at this hour, there was no one else around. He raced down to the beach and plunged into the sea, relishing the feeling of cold water on his skin. He struck out vigorously and swam some distance, taking deep breaths and feeling better than at any time since his return from the Crimea.

As he returned he became aware of Frank, standing on the beach waving to him.

"I just wanted to let you know that the old feller has really gone back to London," he said. "I saw him in a carriage, going by at seven o'clock. Mrs. Jones says there is a train to London at half past seven, so he must have been catching that one."

"Then we have got rid of him!" John exclaimed. "That poor girl can stop being a prisoner in her room."

"Are we going to find somewhere else for her, sir?"

"I suppose that would be an idea – if I could think of anywhere."

In fact he was planning to spend the day with Cecilia.

When they reached the hotel, he ran straight up to her room, hoping to find her alone. She answered the door wearing her dressing gown and again he noticed her lovely hair streaming over her shoulders.

"I have come to tell you that you can relax," he said. "Sir Stewart has taken the train to London."

She clasped her hands.

"Oh, how wonderful! If only he stays there!"

"I am sure he will. When he doesn't find you at his house, he will think of other London houses you might have gone to. Can you think of where he might search?"

"Papa had several friends in London. He might try them first."

"Then we are safe, at least for a while. I wondered if you would care to go swimming with me."

"Oh, I would love to."

"Do you have a costume?"

"No, I ran away in such a hurry, I couldn't even think of swimming."

"I know a shop where you can buy one. I will come back for you in an hour."

John descended for his breakfast and give instructions to the staff. Mrs. Jones told him kindly not to worry about anything, which he interpreted, correctly, as meaning that they could all cope very well without his ignorant interference.

He was whistling happily to himself as he went to call for Cecilia an hour later. But it was Miss Campbell who opened the door.

"I won't need to buy a costume," Cecilia said, "because dear Roseanne is lending me one of hers. And she is coming to the beach with us. Isn't that nice?"

John agreed that it was. He would gladly have dispensed with Miss Campbell's company, but he had spoken sincerely when he had said he was glad that this young lady had a female protector.

He waited for the ladies downstairs, but it was Frank who joined him a few moments later, laden down with baggage.

"Aren't you working in the taproom this morning?" John asked.

"No sir. My orders are to come to the beach with you."

"But I gave you no such orders."

"No, sir, you didn't," Frank said woefully. "But *she* did. She has just given me all the bags to carry. Of course," he added, brightening, "you could always order me to stay here."

"And disobey Miss Campbell?" John asked with a grin. "What a hero you must be, Frank! No, I think you had better come to the beach with us and – er – do whatever she tells you."

"You are a hard man, sir. A very hard man."

The next moment they saw the ladies descending to join them and Frank fell into cowed silence.

CHAPTER SEVEN

Half an hour later the party left the *Paradise Hotel*. John and Cecilia went first, she clinging to his arm and tripping along daintily, clad in a soft blue dress that he thought was enchanting.

Behind them came Miss Campbell. Frank brought up the rear, glaring and puffing under the weight of bags.

When they reached the beach, John hired two bathing machines and he and Frank took one, while the ladies took the other.

"Are you joining us in the water?" John asked his valet. "Or hasn't Miss Campbell given you her orders yet?"

"That's right, kick a man when he's down," Frank observed gloomily. "She didn't say anything, so I am coming in. If she objects I'll – I'll – "

"You'll what?" John asked, fascinated.

"I'll ask you to protect me, sir. After all, I work for you, not her."

"I will do my very best to protect you, Frank," John said, keeping his face admirably straight, "although it may well be beyond my power."

"But you charged the Russian guns at the Battle of Balaclava, sir," Frank pleaded.

"Yes, and having taken part in one suicidally foolish

action, I have no desire to risk my neck in another. It is time you saw some action, Frank."

"Yes, sir."

"Do you possess a costume, by the way?"

"Yes, sir. I used to swim a bit in the lake at home. The butler loaned me his costume and when we left Milton Park, I sort of forgot to give it back to him."

"Admirable forethought! Then let us go into that contraption and make a start."

It was dark in the machine and John found it hard to see what he was doing. Just as he had finished changing, the machine gave a jerk as the horse began to drag it into the sea, stopping when the water was about three feet deep. They heard the sound of the horse being unharnessed and taken away.

"Ready?" John asked Frank.

"Ready as I ever will be, sir."

Frank opened the door which led to the steps down into the water, stood aside to allow his master through, and then followed him down. They swam a few strokes and looked back to the other machine, which had by now reached its place in the water. The horse was just being led away.

After a moment the door opened and they had their first glimpse of a very pretty flowered cap. That was exactly the sort of enchanting creation that Cecilia would wear, John thought contentedly. But the next moment he felt a shock.

The face under the cap was Miss Campbell's.

It was she who descended first, looking cautiously this way and that, to ensure that no disrespectful male eyes were fixed on them. She jumped quickly into the water, but there was still time for John and Frank to observe the deep pink of her costume, plus the fact that her figure was more voluptuous than they had previously suspected.

Frank's eyes were popping out of his head, John was amused to notice.

"Sir," he breathed, awed. "I never realised that she was so – so – "

"Certainly her normal attire does not do her justice," John agreed. "Now, you behave yourself, my lad. You hear me?"

Frank did not answer. He was past hearing anything.

Then Cecilia appeared and John promptly forgot all about Miss Campbell.

Cecilia also wore a pretty flowered cap, very similar to Miss Campbell's, although, to John's entranced eyes, nobody could confuse the two women for a minute. Cecilia was divinely slender, her elegant figure sheathed in a deep blue costume.

Naturally the costume was modest, with a skirt that flared over her hips and came down almost to her knees. Even so, it could not disguise the notion that she was built like a fairy.

Seeing him watching her, she hurried down into the water, but not before John experienced an enchanting glimpse of slim exquisite ankles.

He waved and she swam towards him with easy, confident strokes.

"You are a good swimmer, madam," he said. "I congratulate you."

"I love swimming," she replied. "I bathed in the sea as much as I could when we were living here. It makes me feel free of all the troublesome restrictions in my life, as well as free of my fears."

"You are not going to be afraid today," he stated firmly. "I will not allow it."

Cecilia looked at him, feeling a glow of joy. When he

spoke like that, she felt as if there was nothing to be afraid of in the whole world.

She looked around, rejoicing in the vast expanse of sky and sea and the glorious sense of liberation it gave her. She began to back away from him, further out into the water.

"Not too far," he cautioned at once, reaching out a hand towards her. She evaded him and took another step backward.

"I am a good swimmer," she responded.

He stepped forward, trying to take her hand, but she evaded him again.

"Miss Smith – "

"My name is Cecilia – "

"Cecilia, please be careful – "

"I don't want to be careful. I seem to spend all my life watching out for danger. Now I want to be free."

She moved back quickly, yet her hand was extended to him, inviting him to follow where she led. John accepted the invitation with all his heart, telling himself that he was concerned for her safety, yet secretly knowing that he could not resist joining her.

She began to swim with determined strokes. He followed her, heading out into deep water. Sometimes she would turn and swim backstroke so that she could watch him and make sure that he was following.

She is enchanting, John thought, as she was drawing him ever onward and out to sea. Just as a mermaid might lure her prey after her on a journey to mysterious echoing caves, where the sirens sang. And he would follow to whatever secret unknown destination she led him, because he had no choice.

He was amazed at the way she swam. Women were supposed to be feeble and delicate, but she could move strongly, cleaving through the water with sure swift strokes.

He began by holding back, so as not to overtake her, then realised that he was falling behind and had to put on a spurt to catch her up. She smiled, understanding the game and swimming even faster to tease him.

Way, way out they went, until they seemed to be floating in their own perfect world.

"Cecilia," he called.

She turned and leaned back in the water, watching him with an enigmatic smile.

"I don't think we should go any further," he said.

Her head told her that he was right, but it was as though she had turned into another being, one who could say outrageous things and mean them.

"I am not afraid," she told him. "Are you?"

"Do you know, I am beginning to think that I am a little afraid," he said. "Afraid for you, but also afraid of you. I don't know you any more. It is as though you are no longer a woman, but have become a mermaid."

Her heart leapt at his words and even more at his tone. He sounded like a man bewitched and suddenly she knew that she wanted to bewitch this man more than she wanted anything else on earth. She wanted to charm and enchant him, she wanted to baffle and confuse him. She wanted him to lie awake all night wondering about him – as she had done last night.

She swung away from him, gliding delicately through the water and he followed.

"Stop," he gasped at last. "Have mercy, mermaid. This mere mortal cannot keep up with you."

She took his outstretched hand and they trod water, each gasping and exhilarated.

"You madwoman!" he exclaimed, laughing. "How

could you do such a stupid thing?"

"It is not stupid for me," she cried. "I am a mermaid and I can swim anywhere. I can swim round the world."

"Take me with you," he pleaded suddenly.

The sea and the sky moved into a dizzying spin. For a moment the whole world belonged to her and everything was glorious.

"What – what did you say?" she asked.

"I said take me with you," John repeated with quiet intensity.

He was not aware that his hand had tightened on hers, but Cecilia felt it and her heart soared. Perversely she would not let him suspect.

"I cannot take you with me," she asserted. "We mermaids swim alone and no man may follow us. It is forbidden."

She pulled away from him and dived swiftly, so that he saw a flash of shapely ankle before she vanished into the depths. Instantly he dived as well and felt a moment's panic because he could not see her in the dark blue water.

At last he sensed her gliding past him as though she was indeed the mermaid she had claimed to be. This time he was taking no chances. He put on a spurt and caught up with her, seizing her waist.

Above them the water was pale from the light above. Up and up they climbed until they broke the surface and the sunshine streamed over them again. At first they laughed into each other's eyes, but suddenly they stopped laughing and trod water, looking astonished at what had come over them.

The shore was so distant as to be almost invisible. Overhead the blue sky was empty and the sea stretched far away into the distance. They might have been completely alone in the world with no one to see what they did next.

Slowly John drew her towards him. Her arms enfolded his neck and the next moment he was kissing her, and she was kissing him.

For Cecilia it was her first kiss, except for those that Sir Stewart had forced on her that she had fought so hard to avoid. Secretly she had always dreamed of her first true kiss from a man who had captured her heart and made her want to be his.

Now it was happening and in that one moment she knew that this was the man she had been waiting for. There were so many places she might have gone, in her flight, but some instinct had directed her to the place where he was.

In some dim distant corner of her mind she knew that it was shocking for her to be behaving like this with a man she hardly knew, especially when both of them were so lightly clad. But she could not believe that it was improper when everything inside her reached out to him.

He was the man her heart had chosen, for now and for ever. He was her friend and her protector and now she longed to call him lover and husband.

They drew slowly apart, not releasing each other, still treading water as they drew back slightly to regard each other in a new light.

"Cecilia," he murmured, "forgive me – "

"There's nothing for me to forgive," she interrupted him joyously.

"It was wrong of me to take advantage of you – out here, where you are defenceless – "

She almost laughed aloud. She did not feel defenceless. She felt strong and in control. After all, if was she who had insisted on swimming so far out and he who had followed helplessly. She put her head on one side and looked up at him with teasing humour.

He understood her. It was he who was helpless under her spell. But he knew he must force himself to behave with propriety.

"I – think we should return," he said unsteadily. "You are so lovely that I – I might forget to behave like a gentleman."

She chuckled.

"Now you sound like Papa. He was always talking about acting 'like a gentleman' but I am afraid people always knew that he was not one. You don't have to pretend with me."

Her words forced him to remember that she was ignorant of his rank. She saw him as no more than a hotel manager, and therefore not a gentleman. He was deceiving her.

"I think we should go back," he repeated hurriedly. "We are a long way out."

She sighed.

"Yes," Cecilia agreed reluctantly. "I suppose we must come back to earth."

He did not ask what she meant. He too had felt transported to the stars.

They turned and began to swim towards the land. For the first time Cecilia realised just how far away the shore was. The distance had seemed like nothing when she swam out, full of strength and courage for the adventure.

But now the beautiful moment was over. The sun had vanished behind clouds and an ache of disappointment pervaded her. She was not sure what she had expected to happen, but she felt suddenly sad. The shore seemed to be moving away as she headed for it and she was tired.

"Not much further," John reassured her.

"I suppose you were right," she said. "I should have listened to you. It was too far."

"Do you regret it?" he asked.

She shook her head. There were no words for what she felt or if there were, they were words she could never say to him. She was full of feelings and sensations that she had never known before, and she realised that she would not fully understand them all until she could shut her bedroom door and be alone for a long time, coming to terms with the new life that had begun to unfold for her.

But now she was tiring fast and the shore looked no closer.

"Hold on to me," John urged. "Put your hands on my shoulders."

She did so, floating above him, feeling the strength in his muscles as he forged ahead and the sudden movement of the water beneath her body as he kicked his legs. Now a new sensation pervaded her, that she could rely on John to defend her forever.

'Oh, Papa,' she thought, 'what would you think of me now? You wanted me to marry a Lord and now I have fallen in love with a tradesman. How disappointed you would be! But I cannot help it. I love him more than all the Lords in the land.'

Then she saw something that made her look more keenly.

"Is that rowing boat coming towards us?" she asked.

John raised his head.

"Yes and I think that's Frank rowing," he replied. "And there's Miss Campbell."

Frank had his back to them, but Roseanne faced them and he saw her suddenly lean forward, pointing in their direction. Frank looked back over his shoulder and redoubled his efforts. In a few minutes the boat was beside them.

"Well done, Frank, you are a very welcome sight," John said breathlessly. "We are both tiring a little."

"So I thought, sir. But it's not just that. *He* has come back."

"Come back? You mean Sir Stewart?"

Cecilia gave a little scream.

"Oh, no. He can't have."

"He turned up at the hotel and Mrs. Jones sent a message down to the beach. So I rowed out to collect you. Climb aboard quickly, sir."

John lifted Cecilia high out of the water and Miss Campbell helped her into the boat. Then Frank hauled his master in.

"Heavens!" Cecilia cried. "What am I going to do? Suppose he comes to look for me on the beach. Suppose he sees us land?"

"I have thought of that, miss," Frank said, pointing to some towels in the bottom of the boat. "I brought these. If you lie down we can cover you with them until we reach land and then – then we'll think of something else."

"But you had better lie down at once," Miss Campbell suggested. "We must take no chances."

As she spoke she was drawing towels over Cecilia until she lay, completely covered, in the bottom of the boat. John took one of the oars and he and Frank rowed the rest of the way to the shore, while Miss Campbell lay back, trying to look like a lady of leisure being escorted by two cavaliers.

The two men rowed with their backs to the shore and it was left to her to study the crowded beach for any sign of danger.

"I can't see him," she said. "I think we're in luck – oh, no! There he is!"

Cecilia gave a little scream and pulled the towels further around her.

"Where?" John asked, trying to squint over his shoulder.

"Don't turn round in case he sees your face," Miss Campbell said quickly. "He is walking away along the beach. If we're quick we'll get ashore before he turns back."

They began to row very fast while Miss Campbell scanned the shore.

"Hurry, hurry," she urged. "I can still see him in the distance – he is turning round now – "

They were nearing their bathing machines. As they reached them John leapt out of the boat, helped Cecilia over the side and hurried her up the steps of the first one he came to. He slammed the door, locked it and turned to find her collapsed on the floor, shivering.

"It's all right," he said, dropping down beside her and taking her in his arms. "I will not let him take you."

"He will, he will," she whispered in anguish. "I will never escape him. Wherever I go he will always follow me."

John drew her closer in a gesture of fierce protection.

"You must not talk like that," he stressed. "That is the talk of despair and you are too young and beautiful to despair. Your life must be full of joy and love."

"I used to think so," she said. "But not now. He'll catch me one day, I know he will."

"I will not let him," John declared again aggressively. "I will protect you against anything, I swear it."

She looked up at him with a look of admiration so intense that he was dazzled by the glory of her face. For a long moment he gazed down at her sweet upturned face, fighting the temptation to kiss her. The feel of her body pressed against him was almost shockingly intense. The thin material of her bathing costume provided her with scant covering. He could feel every curve of her soft flesh and the fact that it was wet only increased the sensation.

Horrified, he realised that the same must be true of his own costume, sodden and clinging to him. It was almost like wearing nothing at all.

He was dazed from the sensations coursing through him. He knew that he *had* to kiss her. There was no choice. He drew her closer and closer.

But at the last minute he was stopped by a thunderous noise. It came again and again and now they could hear that it came from outside, as though somebody was hitting the wooden side of the bathing machine with a heavy object. On and on it rumbled and beneath it they could just hear the voice of Sir Stewart, bellowing with rage. No words were discernable, just a furious continuous roar.

"He's here," Cecilia cried in anguish. "Oh, John, what shall we do? Help me."

"Yes – " he said slowly. "Yes – protect you – "

Something strange in his voice made her glance at him quickly and she saw a look in his face that she had never seen before on anyone. It was dark inside the bathing machine and she could see him only dimly. Even so she could see that his face was haggard and strained and his eyes tortured.

"What is it?" she asked urgently. "Tell me, please. Why do you look so terrible?"

But he did not seem to hear her. He was staring into the distance, while the thunderous battering continued on and on, close to them, just outside.

"A man can only do what is in his power," he grated, in a voice that spoke of ghastly inner torment. "But he must do that, even when the world seems full of terror – he must do the best he can."

With a sense of shock, Cecilia realised that he had withdrawn from her into another place where she could not follow. She did not know that place, but she could see his agony. He had vowed to protect her, but now her heart reached out to him and it was she who longed to take care of him.

"What is it?" she begged. "Can't you tell me?"

He turned his terrible eyes onto her.

"It cannot be told," he said hoarsely. "You think you are prepared beforehand, but nothing can prepare you for the noise and the smoke – worst of all is that you know it is all useless. You are there on a fool's errand but you cannot turn back. You have to see it through to the bitter end – only there is no end and there never will be because you will carry the horror with you forever."

"No!" she exclaimed fiercely, seizing hold of him and giving him a little shake. "It won't be with you forever, because I will be there and I will drive it away for you!"

"*Get out of my way!*"

Sir Stewart's bawling voice reached them from outside, increasing their tension. John passed a hand over his eyes.

"I am going out," he murmured.

"You can't," she said frantically.

"I must – protect you – leave it to me."

But she could see that he still was not himself. Anything could happen to him out there.

"No," she begged as he rose to his feet.

"There is no other way – duty – duty – "

Moving vaguely, he made his way to the door. He was going out of the bathing machine, but she knew also that he was going somewhere else. If only she knew where.

As John pushed open the door, Sir Stewart had resumed banging the side of the machine with his stick, but he whirled at the sight of John.

"There you are!" he screamed. "Where is she?"

"I have told him the lady is not present, sir," Frank said. "But he will not believe me."

"Because you are lying," Sir Stewart bellowed in a mad voice. "She's in there. I know it. Let me pass."

He tried to thrust his way past John, who planted himself in Sir Stewart's path.

"Get back," he said. "The lady you seek is not here."

"I will see that for myself. Get out of my way."

"No!" John cried out stoutly.

As his answer Sir Stewart drew a pistol from inside his coat and pointed it straight at John.

"Get out of my way," he yelled.

"No!" John repeated.

Watching him, Roseanne and Frank could see that something strange was happening to him. It was as though he did not realise that the gun was dangerous. He took a step down, then another, his eyes fixed, not on the gun, but on Sir Stewart's face.

"Don't come any closer," Sir Stewart shrieked. "Get back."

John shook his head.

"Towards the guns," he muttered. "Always towards the guns. That is how it has to be."

He came down another step. Thinking he saw his chance, Sir Stewart tried to dodge round him but John stopped him with one hand. His eyes still held a blank stare, but his grip was like steel.

"Get back," he ordered. "Take warning, I will not let you pass."

Sir Stewart tried to break free. When he found John's grip was unbreakable he began to howl with rage. All around them people on the beach were staring at them. Some of them rose to their feet in consternation, but they kept well back, mindful of the gun.

Frank made a lunge at the pistol but Sir Stewart retaliated by aiming it straight at him. But before he could pull the trigger, John uttered a cry that chilled the blood of all who heard it and launched himself on to Sir Stewart, carrying him down to the ground.

For a moment the two men rolled fiercely in the sand while everyone stared, aghast.

Suddenly there was a roar as the gun went off. For a moment they were both still. Then Sir Stewart began to wriggle frantically away, leaving John lying there alone, blood pouring from him.

CHAPTER EIGHT

"John! John! Oh, no – please God, no!"

It was madness to run out of the bathing machine, but when Cecilia heard the shot and the screams from the crowd, nothing could have stopped her. In a moment she was outside, rushing down the steps to fall on her knees beside John and seize him up into her arms.

"No," she wept. "Don't let him die! John! John!"

Everything seemed to swirl around her. Vaguely she heard Frank, calling for a doctor and for help to carry the wounded man back to the hotel.

By a miracle there was a doctor nearby, who had just arrived at the beach, ready to enjoy an afternoon in the sun, but abandoned it when he saw the crisis. He moved Cecilia gently aside and studied John.

"He is losing blood fast," he said curtly. "Where is the hotel?"

"Just over there," Frank informed him, pointing.

"Not too far. Good. Then let's get him inside at once."

He helped Frank lift the patient and the two of them carried John off the beach.

Cecilia followed behind, her whole heart and mind concentrating on John, and how she might be about to lose him just when she was realising that she loved him.

Everything vanished from her mind, including propriety, so that Frank had to turn her back at John's bedroom door.

"We are going to have to undress him, miss," he said, blushing as he spoke and firmly barring her way.

"Come and change out of that wet costume," Roseanne said, guiding Cecilia firmly towards her room.

Roseanne was a tower of strength. She had had the forethought to collect all the clothes from the machine before she left the beach. Now the two girls dried off and helped each other to dress.

"I must go back to him," Cecilia cried frantically. "Oh, if only he is still alive!"

"Of course he is," Roseanne soothed her. "I saw what happened. The wound is only in his shoulder."

"Did Sir Stewart do it?" Cecilia asked bitterly.

"That he did, miss. First of all he banged on the machine with his stick. He was being very nasty, but you should have seen how Frank stood up to him. When Mr. Milton opened the door, Sir Stewart pulled out a gun and waved it at him.

"I heard him shout 'don't come any closer,'" Cecilia said.

"That's right, miss. But Mr. Milton was not afraid of him. He said something – I hardly caught it, he spoke so quietly, but it sounded like, 'towards the guns'. Then he came down the steps, heading straight for Sir Stewart, even though the gun was pointed straight at his chest.

"Sir Stewart tried to push past. Mr. Milton seized him, but he could only reach his free arm, not the one with the gun. Frank made a lunge for it, but that devil pointed the gun at him. I think he would have fired, but Mr. Milton hurled himself onto him. He is a brave man, miss."

"Yes, yes" Cecilia sobbed through her tears.

"Mind you, Frank is a brave man as well."

Cecilia barely heard her. One thought was torturing her.

"He did it all for me. If John dies, it is I who will have killed him."

"But you shouldn't have come running out as you did, miss. That was dangerous."

"I never thought about it," Cecilia replied, in a daze. "I could only think of – him. But it was very foolish of me, I can see that."

"If Sir Stewart had kept his wits about him he could have dragged you off there and then. Luckily he panicked. When he saw what he had done, he made a run for it," Roseanne added with grim satisfaction. "He couldn't get away fast enough, so he never saw you. Let us hope that's the last of him."

"Oh, yes. If only he's too scared to come back. And if only John – oh, Roseanne, let's go quickly and find out how he is."

Together they hurried to John's room, where the doctor was just finishing. Frank let them in, standing back so that Cecilia could see the bed where John lay.

They had removed his bathing costume and now his bare chest was heavily bandaged. He was unconscious and lay very still, his face dreadfully pale, his eyes sunken.

"I have done what I can for him," the doctor announced.

"He will be all right, won't he?" Cecilia pleaded.

"I do hope so. He was lucky in that the bullet just missed his lung, but he has lost a lot of blood. It is best if he remains sedated as far as possible. I have sent one of your servants to the apothecary for something that will keep him quiet – ah, here he is."

Responding to a knock at the door, the doctor took the medicine from the servant outside, saying,

"I am returning home tomorrow morning, so you had better send for the local doctor. The patient is going to need constant care."

"I will show you out and see to your fee," Frank said.

"Thank you for everything," Cecilia breathed fervently.

"My pleasure, madam. And there is no need for a fee. This was an emergency."

When they had left and Roseanne with them, Cecilia crept closer to the bed and dropped to her knees beside John.

"I am here, my love," she whispered. "And I am going to stay here, looking after you until you are well. You are not going to die, because I will not allow it. Do you understand? I am going to keep you safe."

He did not stir. Nor did he give any sign of hearing her. Scarcely daring to breathe, Cecilia leaned closer and softly touched his face with her fingers.

Then she lay down her head and sobbed.

But she only allowed herself a brief moment of indulgence. She raised her head and straightened her shoulders. She was going to need all her strength for John's sake. And she would not fail him.

*

Towards the guns – towards the guns.

John tried to think clearly, but he was surrounded by heat and smoke. It had been madness to charge the guns, but a soldier could not disobey an order and so they all had ridden forward into hell.

The noise inside his head was deafening, but worse than the noise, the heat and the smoke, was the sense of despair and terrifying futility.

His body was racked with pain. He was dying. He knew it and prepared to descend into blackness, but at the last moment a woman's voice had murmured soft words of comfort and her gentle hand seemed to hold him back from the brink.

Now he knew who she was, Florence Nightingale, who had travelled to the Crimea, bringing hope and succour to so many soldiers dying of neglect.

But when he opened his eyes it was not Florence Nightingale whose face hung over him, but Cecilia's. She was pale and he thought he saw tears on her cheeks. Then the night engulfed him again and he closed his eyes. At the last moment he thought he felt a pair of soft lips pressed to his forehead, before he lost consciousness.

This time his sleep was peaceful, as though her presence could drive his nightmares away. He did not know how long he lay there, drifting through dreams, but it seemed like an endless journey.

Sometimes he seemed to be back at home, wandering through the gardens, returning to the place where he had often sat with his mother before she died. Or he would be running through a maze, hearing the voices of his father and brother calling from some other part that he could never find. He had always known that he was excluded from their charmed circle.

Next he was a soldier again, splendid in the uniform of the Light Brigade, brave and cheerful as a new life opened to him. But the new life ended in the smoke and despair of a fruitless charge down the valley to the Russian guns.

Again and again he would reach this point and every time his horror would be driven away by a gentle voice, and an even gentler touch. And once more he would be lulled back to sleep.

*

At last he awoke once more. This time the world was cool and peaceful.

And she was there.

For a long time he looked up into her beautiful eyes, smiling down at him with love and joy.

"Hallo," he said weakly.

"Hallo." Her voice was as soft and sweet as an angel's.

"Have you been here all the time?"

"Yes, I have."

"I thought so. Every time I opened my eyes you were with me and I felt better and fell asleep."

Slowly he raised his hand to his chin, frowning at what he found.

"I have grown a beard. How long have I been here?"

"Four days. We did not want to disturb you by shaving you."

"We?"

"Frank and Roseanne have been wonderful. He is now running the hotel with her help. And she is also helping me to nurse you. She is a tower of strength. They both are."

"What has been happening?" John asked. "I remember nothing after he shot me. What happened to him?"

"He ran away."

At that moment Frank put his head round the door, beaming when he saw that John was awake. Roseanne was just behind him and the three of them told John everything that had happened after he lost consciousness.

"And now I am going to fetch you some nice strong broth," Roseanne said, bustling away.

"How is the hotel doing, Frank?"

"Tip-top, sir. Mr. Dale would be proud of us."

"Proud of you, you mean," John said. He saw that Cecilia was looking puzzled and added, "Robert Dale is a friend of mine and the son of the Mr. Dale you knew. We met in the Crimea. He owns this place."

Roseanne returned with the broth and a message to say that the doctor would be here soon.

"He has been to see you every day since the first doctor left," Frank explained. "He was rather worried when you took so long to recover consciousness – in fact we all were. But all is now well."

The doctor arrived soon after lunch and confirmed Frank's view. Plenty to eat, plenty of rest and plenty of good nursing were his recommendations.

For a couple of days John allowed himself to drift comfortably between sleeping and waking. He gave himself up to this routine, having no strength to do otherwise, but he was also enjoying being cared for by Cecilia. Once he said,

"Did I say anything while I was unconscious?"

"You muttered a good deal, but I didn't understand much. You spoke of guns and smoke and once you cried out. What were you dreaming of?"

"The charge," he replied. "I was in the Light Brigade."

"You were part of the glorious charge?" she gasped.

But at once she knew she had made the wrong comment, for John's face darkened.

"It was not glorious," he scolded her. "It was stupid and pointless. It was not even meant to happen the way it did. The commander who gave the order didn't mean us to charge the guns, but take a different direction entirely, only we could not see the way to go."

He began to laugh harshly.

"Isn't that funny? The 'heroic' charge was a mistake all the time. Did you ever hear of anything so ridiculous?"

"Oh, my dear John," she said, gathering him into her arms.

"There is nobody I can tell," he choked, "because nobody wants to know the truth."

"You can tell me anything. I am sorry I reacted in that stupid way."

"It is how everyone feels. Six hundred and seventy-three men set out, a quarter of them died, and everyone says how splendid. If they only knew.

"Since then I think I have been angry every moment of my life. I lay in the Barrack Hospital full of fury, I left the army and came home and I was angry all the time. Only Robert Dale understood. He once said, 'nothing was ever the same after the Crimea,' and he was right."

"Oh, yes, I remember. You told me that he owns the *Paradise Hotel* and that he gave you the job."

"Which was very trusting of him, since I have no previous experience of hotels."

"Perhaps you need to talk to him rather than me, if he fought though the war with you."

"He is in London now, being 'mine host' at the *White Elephant* in the East End. In truth I would rather talk to you."

But even as he said it, he knew that he no longer needed to talk. It was enough to lie here, resting against Cecilia in the peace that only she could give him.

Their peace was untroubled until the following day, and then it was rudely disturbed.

Frank, working in the bar downstairs, looked up to find a tall, youngish policeman, with a large moustache, advancing on him.

"I am Constable Jenkins," he said. "I understand there was an incident on the beach in which a man was shot."

Frank stared at him.

"But that was four days ago," he said.

"Yes, well – " the constable became rather awkward, "the wheels of justice grind slow but they grind sure."

"What does that mean?" Frank demanded.

"It means – it means that I am here now. The fact is that nobody knew where anybody was. The gunman vanished before we were called and the victim vanished too."

"We brought him here to be tended by a doctor."

"But you didn't tell anyone where you were going, did you? It took a lot of searching to find you."

"What about that madman? Have you found him?"

"The wheels of justice – " the constable stopped under Frank's withering glance. "No, sir, but we will. Is the victim still here?"

"Of course. He's being nursed upstairs."

"I would like to see him."

"I will find out if he is awake." A flash of inspiration made Frank add, "in the meantime, why don't you sample our best ale, on the house?"

"Well sir, strictly speaking I am not supposed – er – "

He faltered into silence as Frank placed a foaming tankard before him.

"I expect the wheels of justice grind a bit dry sometimes," he commented, straight-faced.

"As you say, sir. As you say."

He settled down happily, while Frank sped upstairs and into John's room. He was conscious but weak, lying back on his pillows talking contentedly to Cecilia.

"There's a policeman here," Frank said in a soft, urgent voice. "They have finally come round to doing something, only they haven't caught Sir Stewart."

"That might be just as well for the moment," John said. "If they did catch him he would only bluster and lie and I would rather be a little stronger before I have to deal with his behaviour again."

"But what should I say to the policeman?" Frank asked. "How much should I tell him?"

"As little as possible. Leave him to me. Send him upstairs to me, but give Miss Smith time to hide in her room first."

"Must I?" Cecilia asked.

"We cannot be at ease while that man's on the loose. I do not want this policeman to be able to say he saw you."

"And he won't," Cecilia said decisively. "But I will still be here."

"You are going to hide in the wardrobe?"

"Not at all. I will be standing right here. But he won't see me. Frank, will you ask Roseanne to come up and see me, please? And keep the policeman downstairs for ten minutes."

The two men exchanged glances of total bafflement, but Cecilia's decisive mood had taken them by surprise, and neither felt able to challenge her. Frank obediently walked downstairs and plied Constable Jenkins with more beer, explaining that the patient had only just awoken and would need a few minutes to be ready.

Ten minutes later they climbed the stairs. The constable was not a particularly intelligent man, but he was aware that they were passing the guests' rooms to the upper reaches of the building, where the staff were accommodated.

"Who exactly is the injured man?" he asked Frank.

"What does he do?"

"Mr. Milton is the hotel manager."

Constable Jenkins thought, but did not say, 'not a gentleman, then.'

In answer to Frank's knock they received a faint, "come in." Entering, they saw John Milton looking frail and barely conscious, while a female fussed around him.

The policeman gave her the barest glance, taking in her dark dress and plain white cap, beneath which her hair was drawn back severely. Behind her spectacles, her expression was grim.

The nurse, he thought. And forgot her.

He introduced himself and cleared his throat portentously, preparing to take notes.

"You are – ?"

"My name is John Milton. I manage the *Paradise Hotel*, and for the past week I have been plagued by an idiot who is chasing a woman all over the country and has accused me of hiding her."

"Why should he do that?"

"I am not sure. I think he just goes around accusing everyone in sight. In my opinion he is mad. In fact I have the gravest doubt as to whether the woman exists at all. I think she is a figment of his imagination."

"His name?"

"Sir Stewart Paxton."

A perceptible change came over the policeman. He tensed and looked alarmed.

"Sir Stewart?"

"Yes."

"A *titled* gentleman?"

"Yes, he is a Knight, if you call that a title," John

replied wryly, briefly forgetting his role and speaking from the lofty heights of an Earl.

"I *do* call it a title," said Jenkins indignantly. "I was not told he was a titled gentleman."

"What difference does it make?" John demanded. "He still cannot go around shooting people."

The constable shook his head in puzzlement.

"There is a great deal here that we know nothing about," he brooded.

"For pity's sake!" John exclaimed, exasperated beyond endurance. "A man with a title is exactly the same as any other man. In fact, he is usually worse because he has been raised to think he can do as he likes, and he needs to be shown that it isn't true."

Jenkins stiffened in outrage. *"That's anarchy!"*

It might seem wildly illogical that the policeman would find Sir Stewart more believable because of his minor title, especially with the evidence of a bullet wound before his eyes. But, being born into an Earl's family, John had encountered this attitude too often to be surprised by it. Even Robert, he recalled wryly, had relished his lordly background.

"Call it what you like," he said now, too weary to argue any more.

Jenkins breathed out hard, but evidently decided that it was useless to take the matter any further and returned to his notebook.

"And what is the name of the woman he is seeking?" he asked.

John hesitated. Something warned him that it would be wiser not to give Cecilia's name or any details that might lead to her. While he was trying to clear his head, both men were startled to hear a sharp, *"Hah!"*

"Pardon?" said the policeman, looking around.

"Hah!" repeated the nurse. "Name, is it? Who knows what her name is, since *Sir* Stewart – if indeed he is a 'sir', which I take leave to doubt – gave a different one every time he opened his mouth? And some of them were names no decent woman would own to. There is probably more than one woman and no better than they should be – if they existed. And that man is also no better than he should be."

Laboriously the constable wrote down, '*no better than he should be.*' But then he remembered that he was talking about a titled gentleman and scrubbed it out again.

"Is there anything else you can tell me?" he asked.

"No, there is not," the nurse responded firmly, glaring at him from behind her spectacles. "My patient is tired and you are doing him no good."

"Yes, but – "

"Good day to you, constable."

While he was still trying to think of something to say the formidable young woman opened the door, revealing that Frank was waiting outside.

"The constable is just leaving," she declared.

He made one last effort. "Actually, madam – "

"Good day to you."

The next moment, in some way that he could not have explained, he was standing outside the door which had been firmly shut in his face.

John and Cecilia waited until his footsteps had died away, before giving vent to their feelings, exploding with mirth.

"Come here," John said, reaching out to draw her down to sit on the bed. "And take those horrible spectacles off. And that cap."

"Gladly," agreed Cecilia, tossing them aside and

becoming herself again.

"You were wonderful," John exclaimed admiringly. "I almost believed in your dragon."

"I became angry when I saw how tired you were," she said. "I will not let anyone worry you."

"So now you're protecting *me*?"

"If necessary," she answered, setting her chin proudly.

They looked at each other, neither wanting to speak as they felt a surge of mutual understanding passing between them.

There was a knock on the door. It was Roseanne, bearing a tray with his lunch. John thanked her, but Cecilia could see that his appetite had not improved and he was steeling himself to make the effort to eat.

"Now come along," she said when Roseanne had gone. "You must eat to regain your strength."

"Yes, nurse," he said meekly.

"And I am going to help you," she added beginning to cut up the food into small pieces. "Open."

He obediently opened his mouth and allowed her to feed him.

John had never felt so blissfully content in his life.

CHAPTER NINE

The sensation of peace and happiness lasted, although John had not dared to hope that it would. Cecilia was with him almost all the time and he never, for one moment, found her conversation dull. He had not imagimed it possible that he could find a woman's mind so fascinating. He almost laughed aloud at the irony of these thoughts when she said,

"I like arguing with you. It is so hard for a girl to find someone to talk to sensibly. Mostly people expect us to talk nonsense. If we try to talk about serious things men become offended, as though we had trespassed on territory reserved exclusively for them."

"Then they are very foolish," John mused. "They should treasure a woman for her serious qualities as well as for her beauty."

"Too many of them treasure her for her money," she said with a touch of bitterness.

"You will find the right man," he added gently. "One who loves you for yourself."

There was silence for a moment before Cecilia said,

"You are right, of course you are right, it is love which counts. That is what I want, real love. Love from a man who loves me with his heart and his soul and cares nothing for my money."

"And that man does exist," John assured her. "You

might find him where you least expect."

He checked himself, fearful lest he reveal too much. The feeling for her that was growing within him was too delicate and too precious to be exposed as yet to the light of day.

"It is marvellous you feel like that," she exclaimed, looking at him earnestly. "Some people would think that what we have been saying to each other is a lot of nonsense, but I feel that everything you say comes from your very soul."

"It does," he assured her.

"If only that ghastly man has really disappeared," Cecilia sighed. "It has been like Heaven to enjoy a few days without him turning up all the time."

"Yes," John murmured, his eyes on her. "Heaven."

"Sometimes I think that if I see Sir Stewart again I will just give him all the money on condition he leaves me alone."

"Don't be so stupid," John told her sternly. "Of course you must never do that. Why should he benefit from his wrong-doing?"

He spoke as if he was scolding a small child and Cecilia looked at him in some surprise.

"You sound exactly like the governess who used to look after me," she said, "but I know what you are saying is good sense. So tell me what else I can do. There's nothing. *Nothing*! Unless – "

She tensed suddenly, as a brilliant idea came to her.

"If I had a husband or if he thought I had – that would stop him. Or just a fiancé, so that he knew there was a man to fight him – "

"That would not stop him," John said bitterly. "This man is so desperate for money that he will take any risk, even coming back here and challenging a fiancé. And I wouldn't trust that idiotic policeman to arrest him. *A titled gentleman!* For pity's sake!"

"You sound angry, as though you disliked titles." Cecilia queried him, puzzled. "Is he right? Are you an anarchist?"

"No, although I can think of one or two aristocrats the world could well do without," John responded truthfully. "But it has made me realise how foolish we are to think we can shut out reality for ever. Curse this weakness! I need to be strong enough to protect you. We have to find an idea that will work."

"You are right about a fiancé not being good enough," she responded. "Only a husband will do."

"You're not serious!"

"I would marry the devil himself before that man," Cecilia insisted firmly. "Anyone!"

"Anyone, hmm!" John reflected, seeming to consider the idea seriously. "I suppose there is always Frank."

"Oh, no, Frank is going to marry Roseanne."

"Has he told you so?"

"Of course not. He doesn't know yet. But *she* does. It was really decided on the beach when they were wearing their bathing costumes."

"Yes," John replied thoughtfully, remembering Frank, goggle-eyed at the sight of Roseanne descending from the bathing machine.

"They have been falling more and more in love every day since."

"I must give them a really good wedding gift, as thanks for all they have done," John said, but then immediately fell silent, remembering that he was hard-pressed for money.

How far away his other life seemed now!

As he lay there quietly Cecilia began to move around the room, tidying up.

'She's beautiful,' he thought. 'I can't understand why men worry more about her money than they do about her. Most men would love her because she is pretty and amusing and care little for her money.'

Then he wondered if this was true. He had found, all through his life that if someone had money, whether it was a man or a woman, there was always someone else trying to take it from them.

'Why are men so greedy where money is concerned?' he asked himself.

At once he knew the answer.

The average man never had enough.

Many of those who had fought beside him in the army had told him they were determined, if they survived, that they would have enough money to enjoy themselves for the rest of their lives.

"I never want to go to war again, I never want to quarrel with anyone," one man had said. "I only want peace and quiet."

John could appreciate that. It was how he himself now felt. The idea of a settled home life, with a wife and children, was becoming increasingly attractive.

'Two or three sons,' he mused. 'And perhaps one very pretty daughter.'

Then he laughed.

Until now, he had not thought of being married.

He had only thought about enjoying himself in London and any other city where there were plenty of women and an abundance of amusements for anyone who could afford them.

But something had changed. Now marriage seemed the ideal.

But it would have to be to the right woman, he thought, watching Cecilia through half closed eyes. She must be sweet and charming, with gentle hands and a shining countenance.

In fact she *must* be Cecilia.

Suddenly she stopped what she was doing and whirled around. Her face was full of sudden decision.

"I have been struck with an idea," she proclaimed, "and I must tell you about it now, before I lose my courage."

"Why should you need courage to talk to me?" he asked.

"Because – because it's outrageous – and yet it would be the perfect answer. Only you must not think badly of me."

"I could never think badly of you," he stressed fervently. He held out his hand. "Come here and talk to me."

She advanced hesitantly, then took his hand and let him draw her down to the bed. When she was sitting next to him with her hand clasped in his, he said tenderly,

"Now tell me everything."

"The only thing that can protect me from Sir Stewart is a husband, but where am I to find one?"

"Any man would be honoured to marry you, my dear."

"That is what I hoped you would say, because – because there is only one man I could ask. Only one man I trust completely. And – and that man is you."

As soon as she had finished colour flooded her face. It was a deep, rosy pink and very becoming. John watched her, so entranced by her beauty that at first he barely grasped what she had said to him.

Misunderstanding his silence she began to stammer,

"Oh, forgive me, I shouldn't have said that. You must think me so forward. Please, please don't think badly of me – it is only that I am so desperate – "

"Hush," he said, tightening his hand on hers. "It is just that you surprised me. You must be very frightened to suggest such a venture with a man you hardly know. I fear it might be very difficult for you to free yourself afterwards."

He found he was holding his breath for her answer, and it was a sweet relief when she said,

"But I don't want to free myself. What I am proposing is – is – " she took a deep breath and spoke as though reciting, "an arrangement beneficial to both sides."

John's lips twitched.

"Is that what it would be?"

"People have arranged marriages all the time. Of course, they are usually arranged by someone else, but why shouldn't we arrange our own?"

"No reason, I suppose," he surmised, thinking her more enchanting by the moment. "But are you sure this is what you want and that it would really be 'beneficial' to you?"

"Anything that saves me from marriage to that man is beneficial," she said firmly.

"But that is now. When you are married and no longer in fear of Paxton, there would be many years ahead of you, married to a man who might not suit you at all on better acquaintance. You need more in a husband than a bodyguard."

If only, she thought, she could dare to tell him the truth that her heart reached out to him with love. Surely those enchanted moments they had shared in the water must mean something.

But she had gone as far as she dared. She had risked impropriety by proposing to him, but she could never be the first to confess her love.

"Of course I need more than that," she said, speaking calmly to hide the beating of her heart. "I need a man who is kind and understanding, a man I can talk to and confide in. I know all this is true of you."

John remained silent, struggling with temptation. From the moment she proposed he knew he wanted to accept. But did he have the right to take advantage of her need? If she did not love him but was merely turning to him for protection, what kind of marriage would it be for her? For now he knew that he was falling deeply in love with her.

"Cecilia – " he said, tightening his hands on hers, "if only – "

His head was spinning and he was overwhelmed by memories of their time in the water, when she had been a mermaid leading him into the depths. To live with that enchantment always, to sit with her by the fire in the evening, to see her face in his children – all this was such temptation.

But could it be right to yield to such temptation, no matter how great his love?

"Cecilia – " he started gently and then fell silent, uncertain as to what to say next.

Her face fell. A chill was creeping over her heart. This was not what she had hoped for. She tried to be reasonable. She had taken him by surprise and now she must be patient.

"Of course," she said. "You will need to think it over – "

"I don't need to think," he replied. "I already know my answer – "

"But you must not answer me too quickly," she said. "I have not finished explaining. It must seem to you that all the gain is on my side, so why should you give up your life to protect me?"

"Cecilia – " he said, half laughing and thinking of the delight in her eyes when he would tell her that to offer her his life would be his highest joy.

"In return for your protection," she hurried on, "I will give you everything I possess. You will be completely independent. You could buy your own hotel – "

"My dear, your money is nothing to me."

"I know. I have always known that you were a good man. You could never be like *him.*"

"Sir Stewart?"

"Hush, do not even say his name. He has nothing to do with us. I *know* you are not a fortune hunter, which means that I can tell you how much my dowry will be."

She took a deep breath.

"Two hundred and fifty thousand pounds."

For a moment he was unsure whether he had heard correctly. He had imagined her to have ten thousand, perhaps even as much as twenty.

Two hundred and fifty thousand pounds.

There could not be so much money in the world.

Visions danced before him. His home, restored to its old glory, the gardens beautiful again. He could do so much for his tenants, repair their cottages and advance them loans to improve their stock.

And all he had to do was reach out his hand.

That thought brought his whole bright dream crashing down. She was offering him everything with an eager, trusting soul, not knowing that she was putting temptation in the way of a man desperate for money.

In his torment he recalled her saying that she needed a man who cared nothing for her money.

What would she say if she knew that he had deceived her, claiming her trust while hiding the truth about himself?

A quarter of a million pounds. No man needed it more. And no man was less entitled to take it.

Perhaps one day, when there could be total truth between them. But he must tell her that truth carefully. Instinct told him that this was not the moment to blurt it out. She might not even believe him.

"Let us not hurry with this decision," he said at last. "You honour me by suggesting it, but – "

"But you do not wish to," she answered in a shaking voice.

"Listen to me – "

"You do not need to say anything," she said hurriedly. "You are very kind but I should never have – it was wrong of me."

"No, it wasn't – "

"Please, say no more. Forget I ever – excuse me."

Avoiding his outstretched hand, she darted from the room. John was left clutching his hair and cursing himself for being so clumsy.

Back in her own room Cecilia locked the door and leaned against it, her hands covering her face.

'How could I do it?' she whispered to herself. 'Whatever was I thinking of? To propose marriage to a man – oh, I am so shameless and wicked. I was so sure – but I had no right to be sure. I deluded myself with what I longed to believe. Oh, Heavens, what must he think of me?'

For a long time she paced up and down the room, wringing her hands.

'How can I ever face him again?' she moaned. 'I can't. I must get away from here at once.'

But the thought died at once. If she left the hotel she

might run straight into the arms of Sir Stewart. She had no choice but to stay and face her shame.

'But I don't need to see him,' she thought frantically. 'I will ask Roseanne to nurse him while I work downstairs – oh, no, I cannot do that either. Whatever am I to do?'

For a moment she felt as though she would crack under her burdens, but she forced herself to keep calm. She was strong. She must always remember that. And she never needed strength more than at this very moment.

*

Cecilia did manage to avoid John for the rest of the day, but in the evening she had to go to him with his supper and the pills the doctor had left for him.

His face brightened as soon as he saw her and he said eagerly,

"Thank goodness, I have been so hoping to see you."

"Really? Are you feeling ill? Is there something I can do for you?" she asked politely.

"Cecilia please, you know what I meant. I need to talk to you."

"About what?"

"I may have given you the wrong impression – I want to explain – "

"There is nothing to explain," she replied, giving him a bright smile.

"But – "

"In fact, I have no idea what you are talking about. Enjoy your supper."

With those words she whisked herself out of the room, leaving him facing a blank door.

John wanted to bellow aloud at his own clumsiness.

'I should have accepted her offer, then told the truth

and offered to release her,' he groaned. 'Instead I did everything about as stupidly as I could. I must put this right.'

He tried to struggle out of bed, but almost at once he collapsed onto the floor. Frank, entered the room at that moment and yelled, *"Sir!"* and hurried to help him.

"Get into bed, sir," he ordered, guiding him firmly backwards.

"Frank I have to get well fast," John said, breathing hard. "I am useless like this."

"You cannot hurry these things, sir."

"I have to hurry them, dammit! She isn't safe."

Before he could say more they heard the light step of the doctor on the landing outside and the next moment he was in the room.

Dr. Sedgewick was in his thirties, with a plain face and a friendly manner. He came twice a day to inspect John's wound and pronounce it healing well.

"I was just passing and I thought I would look in," he said cheerfully. "How are you?"

"Not too good," Frank said at once. "He just fell on the floor."

The doctor tut-tutted and took out his thermometer.

"Halloo!"

"What's that?" Frank said, frowning at the sound of a voice bawling from below.

"Anyone there?"

"It's that useless policeman," John groaned. "You had better go and see him."

"I think he's coming upstairs, sir," said Frank.

Sure enough, they could hear heavy footsteps and the next moment the door burst open and Constable Jenkins stood there. He was frowning.

"So there you are!" he declared aggressively.

"Yes, here I am," John said. "As you knew perfectly well."

"I thought you might have gone on the run."

"Why should I do that?"

"I have been talking to Sir Stewart."

"You have found him? Thank heavens! I hope he is under lock and key."

"No. I said I have been talking to him, and I've learned a thing or two. It seems you abducted his ward and carried her off with foul designs."

"I told you what he was claiming – "

"Sir Stewart is a titled gentleman," Jenkins stated stiffly. "I hope you are not going to claim that I should disbelieve a member of the aristocracy."

Frank made a rude noise which exactly expressed John's own feelings.

"Even if I did – which I didn't – " John said with heavy irony, "that still would not entitle him to blow a hole in me."

"You launched a vicious attack on *Sir* Stewart, forcing him to defend himself," Jenkins recited.

"Is that what he says?"

"That is *Sir* Stewart's accusation, sir, which I am here to investigate. I have to tell you that I take the matter very seriously."

"You didn't take my master's injury seriously," Frank complained. "It took you four days to come here."

"I would not advise you to get clever with me, my lad," Jenkins responded loftily. *"Sir* Stewart says – "

"For pity's sake, stop saying *Sir* Stewart in that ludicrous manner," John begged. "You only believe him because he has what you fondly imagine is a title and if that is all it takes to impress you, let me give you another one. Earl Milton."

"I don't know what you mean by that."

"I mean that I am an Earl," John fumed. "Lord Milton of Milton Park in Yorkshire and since an Earldom is four steps up from a Knight, I suppose you can assume that I am four times as truthful as that blithering booby that you should have arrested."

Jenkins observed him for a moment and then began to shake his head with mirth.

"Very good, very good," he said. "Clever of you to have thought of that on the spur of the moment, but we in the police force aren't so easily fooled. An Earl! Hah! Oh, yes, very good! An Earl, running a hotel."

"I took it on as a diversion," John snapped through gritted teeth.

"It is true," Frank said. "He is an Earl."

"Oh, yes, you would say the same as him, wouldn't you?" Jenkins said triumphantly. "You are an accomplice. I have a good mind to arrest you as well for the offence of mocking Her Majesty's Constabulary."

"Some things are beyond mockery," muttered the doctor, who had not spoken before.

Now he rose to his feet.

"Get out of here, Jenkins," he said, "and stop making an ass of yourself. You cannot arrest this man, he is too ill to be moved."

The constable hesitated. It was clear that he knew Dr. Sedgewick and was in awe of his authority only a little less than if he possessed a title.

"I have my duty to do, sir. This man is under arrest. I further demand that he produce the young lady concerned."

"I don't have the young lady," John protested angrily.

"In that case, sir – "

Jenkins produced a pair of handcuffs.

"Get out!" cried the doctor, rising to his feet. "Get out at once or I will throw you downstairs myself!"

Jenkins paled and took a step towards the door.

"I have my duty to do – "

"Get out!"

Jenkins took another step back, pointing at John, and saying, "consider yourself under arrest."

Then he fled.

"He will be back," said the doctor angrily. "Is there anyone who can vouch for you, my Lord?"

"Robert Dale could, but he is in London."

"I will go and fetch him," Frank offered.

"You can't. If you are not here who will protect – " John stopped.

"Who will protect the young lady?" the doctor asked sympathetically.

John nodded silently.

"I think I had better go downstairs and see what he's up to," Frank suggested.

"Yes, let's make sure he is off the premises," added Dr. Sedgewick.

John watched them go, mad with frustration at not being able to accompany them. At last, unable to bear the suspense any longer, he crawled painfully out of bed and staggered to the window.

He was always glad that he had done so, otherwise he might have missed a scene that gladdened his heart.

In the gathering dusk he saw Sir Stewart emerge from the hotel entrance, accompanied by Constable Jenkins whose head was bent towards him deferentially.

Suddenly Sir Stewart roared, *"There she is!"*

At that moment a female figure hurried towards the gate. She wore a long cloak with a hood that enveloped her head, so that it was impossible to see her face. But she was Cecilia's height, and from the way she moved, she was young and athletic.

John ground his nails into his palms as he watched the impending disaster. Sir Stewart and Jenkins rushed at her and seized her fiercely. The girl struggled frantically, but she was no match for the two of them.

"Got you!" Sir Stewart roared triumphantly. "That's an end of your wandering, my lady. Now you will come home with me and behave yourself."

"Help!" shrieked the girl. "Help! Kidnap!"

Her cries brought several of the guests out from the hotel, but they backed off when they saw the policeman's uniform.

"Keep clear," Jenkins intoned. "This woman is a desperate runaway, who has been properly apprehended by lawful authority. *Ow!"*

This last noise was produced by a well-aimed heel landing on his calf. The next moment Sir Stewart had seized the hood, pulling it back to reveal the girl's face.

It was Roseanne.

John clutched the window sill to stop himself shaking with relief. The commotion below grew louder. Frank and the doctor had joined the fray.

"Who is this woman?" Sir Stewart bawled. "Where is my ward?"

"But isn't she – ?" Jenkins stammered

"No, she isn't," Frank said grimly. "This is Miss Campbell, my fiancée and if you don't take your hands off her this minute I will make you both very sorry."

"And I will help him," growled the doctor. "Clear off Jenkins and stop making an idiot of yourself."

"Where is she?" Sir Stewart howled. "Where is she? Constable!"

But Jenkins had taken the better part of valour and vanished.

Roseanne took advantage of Sir Stewart's agitation to free herself from his grasp, aiming another kick as she did so, which made him double up. He seemed about to protest further, but thought better of it and limped away.

The doctor followed him to the gate, before turning back just in time to see Roseanne and Frank in each other's arms. He grinned and waved up to the window, where he had noticed John. This made the loving couple look up too, beaming with delight.

After a moment they rejoined John in his room.

"Congratulations," he said. When did you propose, Frank?"

"Five minutes ago," he said, looking slightly stunned. "When I called her my fiancée – well, I've been thinking for some time, but the sight of that brute – "

"Cecilia always said it would happen," John commented.

"I will go and tell her," Roseanne said, speeding away.

But she came back a few minutes later, her face pale and worried.

"She's gone!" she exclaimed.

"She can't be," John said. "She must be hiding in her wardrobe – "

"She isn't. I have looked everywhere. There is no sign of her, and her bag has gone. She has run away."

CHAPTER TEN

Hidden under the trees, protected by the gathering darkness, Cecilia watched the dramatic scene in the yard.

She saw Roseanne fool Sir Stewart and Constable Jenkins and the two men take themselves off, humbled. She watched with pleasure as Frank and Roseanne threw themselves into each other's arms and their return to the hotel, followed by the doctor.

Only when everything was completely quiet did she slip out and walk to the gate. Looking to the left she could make out Jenkins and Sir Stewart in the distance. As soon as they had turned a corner out of sight, she turned to the right and began to run.

After a while she found a cab and hailed it.

"The railway station, please."

All the way to the station she sat well back in the cab, grinding her fingers into her palm, terrified that the last train to London might have gone.

But she was in luck. The London train was still in the station and she was just in time to climb aboard. She would travel to London, perform the task she had set herself and then hide away forever with her shame.

He was an Earl.

Listening outside John's door, she had heard

everything he said and had known at once that he was speaking the truth.

Cecilia, an ordinary girl, had proposed marriage to an Earl. He had let her down gently, too kind to say that a great aristocrat did not marry someone like herself. But the truth was that she had committed a horrible *faux pas* and felt ready to die of embarrassment.

When she thought how she had offered him money to buy his own hotel she could have screamed. And the amount – a quarter of a million pounds – seemed enormous to her, but was probably nothing to him.

How it must have amused him to know that a tradesman's daughter could think herself fit to be his wife! It was lucky that she was alone in the carriage, as the tears began to pour down her cheeks.

She remembered the dismissive way he had spoken of Sir Stewart's title and his air of indifference to titles generally. That should have warned her that he was no common hotel manager. He had said that he had taken on the job as a diversion. There was no accounting for the escapades great Lords regarded as diversions.

Then she remembered the day they had swum together, that magic hour in the water when the whole world seemed hers for the taking. It had seemed so beautiful, but the truth was that he was an Earl, passing the time with a girl far below him on the social scale. And she had embarrassed him by thinking it meant something.

If only she could find a way to stop loving him, but it was too late for that. She would perform this service for him, before hiding in some place where he could never, never find her.

At last the train drew into the station. She dismounted stiffly to search for a cab. Luckily the first cabman that she saw looked kind and fatherly.

"Can you take me to the *White Elephant*?" she asked. "It's an alehouse."

"Can you give me some kind of an address?"

"I only know that it is in the East End."

"But that's a big place."

"Oh, no!" she cried. "I simply have to go there. I cannot let anything stop me now."

"You jump into the cab miss and I'll see what I can find out."

She sat trembling in the cab while he climbed down and vanished for a moment. When he returned he was looking more cheerful.

"That's all right. One of the other cabbies went there only yesterday and he directed me. I know the place, but it isn't suitable for a young lady like yourself."

"Oh, but I must go," she repeated frantically. "Please, you cannot imagine how important it is to me."

"Well," he replied doubtfully, "if I'm with you I suppose it may be all right."

In a moment they were on their way, rumbling through the streets of London which were growing more and more lively. People were going to the theatre and to dinner parties. Lights shone from windows, glimmering on the pavements and cobble stones. Everywhere Cecilia looked she saw good cheer and happiness, contrasting bitterly with the deep ache in her heart.

Gradually the streets changed, becoming shabbier, although there were still lights and the sounds of song and laughter.

"Here we are," announced the cabman at last, drawing up behind a large alehouse. "It looks as though they're just throwing everyone out. Maybe the person you want isn't here?"

"Oh, yes, he's the landlord. Mr. Robert Dale."

"What does he look like?"

"I don't know, I have never seen him before."

"In that case, come on and stay close to me."

Taking a firm grip on her hand, he assumed a scowl, calculated to deter any man too attracted by her fresh beauty and they invaded the building, heading straight for a plump, comfortable looking man behind the bar.

"I am looking for Mr. Dale, the landlord," the cabman asked.

"I am Robert Dale," replied the man.

"There's a young lady here, wants to speak to you urgently."

"Please, it's very important," Cecilia pleaded. "Are you really Mr. Robert Dale?"

"I am?"

"You own the *Paradise Hotel* in Brighton?"

"I do."

"And you were in the Crimea with Lord Milton?"

"Now, how did you know he was a Lord?" Robert asked. "He wanted it kept a secret."

"And he did, but now he is in trouble and he needs you."

"Well, if you are a friend of his Lordship, you are a friend of mine. Come inside."

"How much do I owe you?" Cecilia asked the cabman.

"One shilling and sixpence, please ma'am," he said.

She paid him and added a generous tip, so that he scratched his head and wondered just what kind of young lady this really was. Then she followed Robert Dale into a back room, where he sat her down, ordered his housekeeper to bring her some refreshment and said,

"Now tell me exactly what's wrong."

*

"Sir, how often do I have to stop you getting out of bed?" Frank asked, hurriedly setting down the jug he was carrying and hurrying across to John.

"I have to get up," John said, rising to his feet, clutching at the chest of drawers.

"No sir, you must stay where you are, until you are stronger."

"But I have to find her, can't you understand?"

"Sir, we looked everywhere for her last night. She has vanished. She probably caught a train out of here. That means she's safe by now, where Sir Stewart cannot touch her. It's the best thing for her, sir."

John fell back on the bed, exhausted.

"I suppose you are right," he sighed. "But not to know where she is – to be unable to help her – "

"But at least, if we don't know where she is, neither does Paxton." Frank observed. "If he can't find her here he may even go away and – hallo, what do I see?"

He was looking out of the window.

"*They* are here," he groaned.

"They?"

"The devil and the idiot," Frank replied, not considering any further explanation necessary.

"In that case, it is lucky that she *has* vanished," John said, trying to feel pleased about it.

A moment later Jenkins and Sir Stewart burst into the room.

"Right! You've had as long as I am going to give you," the policeman proclaimed. "John Milton, I arrest you on a charge of abduction. You will receive a long prison sentence, I dare say."

"Unless you admit the truth," Sir Stewart added with a sneer. "This is your last chance. Hand over my ward now, and I will forget the charges."

"I have no idea where your ward is," John answered, slowly and deliberately. "And if you were not such a fool, you would recognise the truth when you hear it."

"Constable, do your duty," Sir Stewart bawled.

Delighted at the chance to do something at last, Jenkins pulled out a pair of handcuffs and advanced on John.

"Where is he? Where's his Lordship?"

The thunderous but cheerful voice in the corridor outside made them all freeze and look towards the door. The next moment it was flung open and Robert Dale stood on the threshold. As soon as he saw John he darted forward and dropped to his knees beside the bed.

"It is so good to see *your Lordship* again," he declared. "I have been a little worried about you being left to manage the *Paradise Hotel*, so different from *Milton Park*, and everything an *Earl* must be used to. And now I see that some common felon has wounded you – *Oh, my Lord!"*

He said the last words with a fervour that made John's lips twitch. At first he had been disconcerted by Robert's theatrical behaviour, but then he realised that his friend had carefully worded his speech for Jenkins's benefit and it was having an effect.

"Your Lordship?" Jenkins echoed. "Milton Park?"

"Of course," Robert said, rising to his feet. "This is Earl Milton of Milton Park."

"A likely story!" Sir Stewart scoffed.

"I knew him in the war," Robert said. "He wasn't an Earl then, just an 'Honourable', Major John Milton of the Light Brigade. He has been awarded a Victoria Cross, one of the new medals that the Queen distributed last year. He is a hero, you see."

He turned on Jenkins, who was gawping.

"You know me, don't you, Jenkins. We met when I came down here six months ago, to visit my father, who owned this place before me."

"Oh, yes," Jenkins replied uneasily. "I remember."

"Then you know who I am. And when I say that this is Earl Milton, you can believe me."

"An Earl," Jenkins gasped.

"I tried to tell you," John observed mildly. "How lucky Robert happened to turn up, at this very moment!"

"This is all very nice and cosy," Sir Stewart raged. "But where is my ward?"

"I do not know," John sighed.

"But I do," Robert said unexpectedly. "It's no accident that brought me here, my Lord. A young lady came to fetch me at my ale house, the *White Elephant*. She said I was the only one who could establish your identity. So I came here. But I left her in London, because she felt safer there."

"The *White Elephant*," Sir Stewart said with a kind of snarling pleasure.

"Yes, but she's not there now. She said she would stay at a hotel. Only she didn't say which one, so you will have quite a few to look through."

"I will find her!"

"Here, what about putting him under lock and key?" Frank demanded of Jenkins. "After all, if Lord Milton is an Earl then he is the one telling the truth, eh?"

It was always possible that Jenkins might spot the fallacy in this reasoning, but experience of the constable's mental processes made this unlikely.

"Yes," Jenkins agreed. Turning to Sir Stewart he

declared, "You are under arrest for the attempted murder of Earl Milton of Milton Park, VC and Honourable."

Sir Stewart swore with contempt and made a dash for the door, but Frank and Robert reached it before him. Jenkins followed up with the handcuffs and in a moment he was helpless, being dragged off to the Police Station with Frank's help.

"Robert, thank you with all my heart," John said. "I do not know what I would have done if you hadn't arrived to save me."

"Don't thank me. Thank the lady. She was very brave and determined."

"How is she? Did you leave her looking well?"

"I didn't leave her at all. She came here with me. Why do you think I told that maniac she was in London? Because she isn't."

"You mean – she is here at the *Paradise Hotel*?"

"Wait."

He walked to the door and opened it a crack, looking out into the corridor. Then he ushered somebody in and tactfully disappeared.

"Cecilia!" John cried joyfully, opening his arms.

But instead of rushing to him, she held back and seemed nervous.

"I am glad to see you well, my Lord."

"My Lord? Whatever are you talking about? We were never that formal with each other."

"No, but I didn't know who you were. You should have told me."

"Why? I was trying to get away from all that."

"You were playing a game, but – it wasn't kind to – to – "

"To what?" he asked, growing more astonished by the minute.

"Never mind," she said hurriedly. "I am so glad everything has worked out well."

"All because you did something wonderful for me, going all that way to find Robert and tell him I needed him. But what I don't understand is how you found out who I was. Did Frank tell you?"

"No, I was just outside your door, listening. I remembered you had once told me about Robert Dale and the *White Elephant*. So I slipped away at once. I waited in the yard until I saw Sir Stewart leave – I saw what Roseanne did, too. Isn't she marvellous?"

"Marvellous," he agreed, his eyes fixed on her face.

"When they had gone, I slipped away and caught a cab to the railway station."

"You did that for me?"

"I just wanted you to be safe. Now it seems that you are and so it is time I departed."

"Why? We have a lot to talk about. Cecilia, please come closer."

He held out his hand and gradually she came closer, when he could seize her hand and pull her down until she was sitting on the bed next to him.

"Tell me what's wrong," he said gently.

To his astonishment, he could feel her shaking.

"Cecilia, my dearest, whatever is the matter?"

"You must not call me your dearest – although I know you are only being kind. But I do understand."

"Understand what?"

"Why it was wrong of me to propose to you. I did not know you were an Earl, but of course now I see why you could not marry me."

"Can you?" he asked blankly. "I wish you would tell me. There is one reason that *might* prevent our marriage, but since it is known only to me, you cannot be talking about that one."

Cecilia frowned, not knowing what to make of his statement.

"I do not understand," she started slowly. "I only know that you are an Earl and I am a tradesman's daughter. If I had known, I would never have asked you to marry me, because of course it is inappropriate, and it is what you meant when you said we must not hurry the decision. You were only seeking a kind way to let me down – "

"Cecilia," he said, unable to endure any more, giving her a fond little shake, "please stop trying to read my mind. You are totally wrong in everything you are thinking."

"But you were going to refuse me, weren't you?"

"Only for a while, just until I could explain something to you that would have made all the difference to your decision."

"But you gave me the clue, didn't you? When you said my money meant nothing to you. How could my paltry little sum mean anything to you, when you must have so much more?"

"I have nothing!"

She stopped and stared at him.

"What do you mean? You are an Earl."

"My darling, if you think you will be marrying into money, you will be in for a shock. I am penniless. Yes, I do own a great estate, but it is encumbered with debt and I have rented it out because I need the money. I have managed to make some improvements, but much more needs doing. Your money would be a godsend to me. So I simply had to refuse. Do you understand?"

"No," she replied blankly.

"I mean that I could not say yes at that moment. First I knew that I must explain everything to you, that I was little better than a fortune hunter, not telling you of my need. To have accepted you then would not have been honest."

She was looking at him in such total bafflement that he wondered if she had fully understood. He held his breath, waiting for her response. When it came, it took him by surprise.

"What utter nonsense!"

"Cecilia – "

"Why can men never see things clearly? You need money and I am offering it to you. Why cannot you simply accept what I am offering, without doing a little dance around it, trying to find difficulties?"

"But there are difficulties," he pleaded. "They are called honourable scruples."

"Piffle to honourable scruples," Cecilia declared calmly. "Of course you are not a fortune hunter. I know what one looks like. Sir Stewart taught me that. Do you think I can see no difference between you and him?

"If you wanted to marry me, you should have said so there and then. Instead you made excuses, because you don't want to marry me. You do not care about me. You would not marry me even though you really need to. That is how little you care!"

Thoughts whirled through John's head – how unreasonable she was being – how unjust – why couldn't she see things sensibly – ?

But then John realised that words were useless. There was only one way to settle this problem.

Grasping her swiftly, he pulled her hard towards him and covered her mouth with his own. For a moment Cecilia raised her hands as if to push him off, but she instantly relaxed and seemed to melt into his arms.

As he felt her warm to him, John tightened his grip, enveloping her in such a powerful, passionate embrace that could leave her in no doubt of his feelings.

Cecilia was in a Heaven of delight. The pressure of his lips on hers answered all her questions.

"I love you," he murmured. "Do you follow me? I love you. That is why I could not agree to marry you. I did not feel that I had the right."

"You have every right," she answered dizzily. "I give it to you."

"In that case, my loved one – will you marry me?"

"Oh, yes," she sighed blissfully. "Oh, yes, yes. I love so you much and it broke my heart when I thought we could never be together."

"Then you will take me, penniless as I am?"

"I am thrilled that you are penniless. It means I have something to give you."

"You do have something to give me, but it certainly is not money. It is your sweetness, your great heart, your lovely face with truth shining from your eyes. Give me those treasures, my darling, and that is all I shall ever need for the rest of my life."

*

They set the date for their wedding day as soon as possible. The doctor began allowing John out of bed for a little longer each day until, after two weeks, he was ready.

"But will we be able to marry while I am still six months away from my twenty-first birthday?" Cecilia asked worriedly.

"I think you can leave that to me," Dr. Sedgewick replied. "The local pastor is my uncle. Let me explain matters to him."

The pastor came to see them the next day at the *Paradise Hotel*. He seemed to understand a good deal about the situation, such as that Cecilia's father was dead. But when she tried to mention a guardian he became mysteriously deaf.

"Is your mother also dead?" he enquired kindly.

"Yes."

"Then, since both your parents are dead, there is nobody you need to ask for consent."

"But – "

"I think that covers everything. I look forward to seeing you on your wedding day."

He bustled away, leaving John and Cecilia gazing at each other in delight. Then they threw themselves into each other's arms.

"Nearly there, my darling," he whispered. "Just a little longer and we will be safe."

As the great day approached they were both on tenterhooks, just waiting for something to happen to spoil their joy.

And then something did.

Two days before the wedding Dr. Sedgewick looked in, his face full of concern.

"I am sorry to inform you that Sir Stewart has been granted bail," he announced heavily.

Cecilia gave a little scream.

"But we were told that he was refused bail," John agonised.

"Yes, but he appealed against the decision and bail was granted this morning. I think he must have bribed somebody."

"And he will come straight to the *Paradise Hotel*," Cecilia cried.

"Yes, so I think the best course is for you not to be here. Come and stay at my house for the next two days. Then he will not be able to find you until it is too late."

They agreed willingly and completed the journey without mishap, although Cecilia's heart was beating fearfully.

'Please dear God,' she prayed, 'do not let anything happen now. I could not bear it.'

John was reluctant to make a run for it. He would have preferred to remain and face Sir Stewart in a more manly fashion. But he knew he was not yet strong enough for such an encounter, so he yielded for Cecilia's sake.

On the morning of the wedding they travelled to the church together, since he would not allow her out of his sight for a moment. Dr. Sedgewick travelled with them, prepared to give the bride away.

Cecilia looked glorious in her white lace gown and veil.

'Like a sweet dove,' John thought, gazing at her with adoration.

Frank and Roseanne were waiting for them at the church. So was Robert who had travelled to Brighton to be the best man.

It was a tiny church and when some of the local citizens noticed that fashionable people in expensive clothes were to be married, they began to tiptoe into the church and stood at the back, full of curiosity.

The vicar took up his position and the service began.

But he had only uttered a few words when the one voice everyone dreaded to hear, howled,

"Stop this wedding! It is illegal."

And there he was, their nightmare, striding down the aisle with two policemen at his back. One of them, John noticed bitterly, was Constable Jenkins.

"Arrest that man," Sir Stewart shouted. "My ward is under age and he is marrying her without my consent."

Jenkins approached, bearing handcuffs, his eyes full of satisfaction at getting the better of the man who had outwitted him.

But before he could reach John the church was rent by a scream, and then another. Scream after scream rang through the building with a terrible cry of –

"Murderer! Murderer! Murderer!"

The two policemen turned to see an elderly woman, thin and frail, totter down the aisle, pointing at Sir Stewart.

"Murderer!"

"Don't talk nonsense," Jenkins began.

But the other constable silenced him, saying,

"Do you mean that Sir Stewart Paxton has killed someone?"

"I don't know his name," the woman wailed. "But I saw him commit murder. It was a year ago, and I had been to London to visit my daughter. On the way back the train was derailed. I was thrown out and lay stunned. When I came to myself I saw two men near me. One was lying on his back, covered in blood and the other was kneeling over him.

"He was saying something. I couldn't hear the words, but he spoke with a kind of savage, wolfish glee that was terrible to behold. Then he put his hand over the other man's face and pressed down hard. His poor victim struggled and fought but he wasn't strong enough, and at last he lay quiet. Murdered.

"I must have passed out because I remember no more.

When I awoke, doctors had arrived and were carrying people away. The two men were both gone. I thought I must have dreamed it. I wanted to believe that. But that devil's face has lived with me ever since.

"I prayed that I might never meet him again. But now I have and I will be silent no longer." She pointed wildly at Sir Stewart. "That is the man."

"Don't believe her," Sir Stewart screamed. "She's a babbling old fool."

"No, she isn't," Cecilia cried. "The man he killed was my father!"

There was a click. Sir Stewart looked down to find himself in handcuffs.

"I think we had better go to the Police Station," said the young policeman, ignoring Jenkins's protests. "And you will have to come too," he added to Cecilia, "and make a statement about what you have just said."

"But this is my wedding," she cried.

"Surely we might be allowed half an hour to finish the ceremony," the vicar pleaded. "Then the bride and groom can join you later."

"Do I have your word?" the policeman asked, looking around.

"Their word, and mine," the vicar declared firmly.

"And mine," said Frank.

"And mine," Roseanne chimed in.

"And mine," joined in Robert.

"And mine," agreed the doctor who, being a local had recognised the constable. He added in a low voice,

"Be decent about this, Tom, and I will forget that fee you owe me."

The constable grinned and nodded. Then, holding firmly on to his prey and refusing to be disconcerted by Sir

Stewart's mad struggles, he hauled him out of the church, beckoning kindly to the old woman to follow.

Cecilia and John looked at each other, their eyes brimming with joy and relief.

"Nothing can stop us now," he told her.

"Nothing in the world," she sighed. "Oh, John, I love you so very, very much."

"And I shall love you all my life. We have at last found our *paradise on earth*."

The vicar coughed.

"Perhaps we should continue," he suggested.

Then, as they turned to face him, he lifted up his voice and began speaking the words they both longed to hear.

"Dearly beloved, we are gathered together to witness the marriage of this man and this woman – "